Lord of Chance

ERICA RIDLEY

ISBN: 1943794049
ISBN-13: 978-1943794041

This is a work of fiction. Names, characters, places, and incidents are the product of the author's imagination or are used fictitiously. Any resemblance to actual events, locales, or persons, living or dead, is purely coincidental.

Chapter 1

Scotland, 1817

Mr. Anthony Fairfax might not be the lord of a manor, but he was king of the gaming hells. Or had been. Anthony glanced at his pocket watch. He should be resuming his throne at any moment. His luck was already turning back around, right here in a humble inn on the Scottish border. And Anthony knew why. He slid another look toward a certain young woman seated alone in the shadows.

Making her acquaintance was almost as tempting as winning the next hand of three-card Brag.

To feign disinterest in the twitches and tells of the other three men at the card table, Anthony lifted his untouched glass of brandy to his lips and leaned back in his chair. Careful to keep a subtle eye on the other gamblers, he glanced about the inn's surprisingly well-appointed salon while he waited his turn.

This particular posting house was a bit dear, given the unpredictable condition of Anthony's purse, but he'd chosen it for that very reason. Rich guests meant higher profits at the gaming tables.

Bored gentlemen—after all, who stopped at a small village on the border between Scotland and England save those on a long, dusty journey?—meant virtually every soul present had wandered into the guest salon after supper to be entertained for a moment or two. Drivers. Gentlemen. Ladies.

For Anthony, the most interesting of all was the intriguing woman in the corner. She drank nothing. Spoke to no one. Seemed uninterested in the bustle of life about her. Yet he knew she was not.

Light from a nearby candle reflected in her eyes every time she looked his way.

Anthony was certain she was the catalyst for his phenomenal luck this evening. A rush of hope filled him. As a lifelong gambler, he was accustomed to both long stretches of near-invincibility as well as dry spells of dashed fortune. From the moment he'd laid eyes on this mysterious woman, every hand he was dealt contained at least a flush or a run.

She was his talisman. His saving grace.

Her moss-colored gown was simple muslin, but the blood-red rubies about her neck and dangling from her ears indicated wealth. A nondescript bonnet bathed her face in shadow. Were it not for a rogue ringlet slipping out the back, he would not have known her hair was spun gold.

"Fairfax?" prompted Leviston. "You in?"

"Absolutely." Anthony placed a dizzying sum of money on the corner of the table. Thirty pounds was more than he'd seen in months—and far more than he could afford to lose. But with Lady Fortune gazing in his direction, he knew he could not fail.

Mr. Bost, failing to hide his smug expression, tossed his final cards onto the table, face up. Mr. Leviston and Mr. Whitfield groaned as they displayed their cards.

As Anthony had expected, their cards were no match for his. Not tonight. He turned over his straight flush without fanfare.

Bost gasped in dismay. "You are positively beggaring me tonight, Fairfax!"

Anthony gazed back impassively as he tucked his winnings into his purse. He knew a thing or two about being beggared. It was what had chased him from London to Scotland—but only temporarily. He *would* recover his losses. Every penny.

Beau Brummell might be able to hide in France for the rest of his life, but Anthony had friends and family in England. People he loved dearly and would miss dreadfully. He straightened his shoulders. London would welcome him back with open arms once his vowels were paid. A few more big wins, and his IOUs would be a distant memory.

Tonight was the night. He could feel it. Fate had been on his side from the moment Leviston had suggested a game of three-card Brag. Anthony could not possibly have resisted.

He had always preferred games of chance over

strategy. His strength was not in counting cards or doing figures, but in being incredibly lucky. Any gambler experienced periods of soaring highs and devastating lows but, in Anthony's case, fortune favored him so often that his winnings at the gaming tables had been his family's sole income for years.

True, he had also suffered agonizing losses but, as any gambler knew, a windfall was always a mere turn of the cards away. Tonight, in fact.

All he needed was one big win.

Whitfield shook his head. "Demme, I should never have believed the rumors of your luck running out. You're unsinkable! Think you'll ever retire from the gaming tables and leave a few pence for us mortals?"

"Never!" Anthony twisted his face into a comical expression of horror.

Chuckling, Whitfield gathered the remaining cards and began to shuffle.

Anthony sent a quick smile toward his shadowy Lady Fortune. She was his charm, his muse. Her power was immeasurable. He had won that last round simply because she'd gazed upon him.

"I see our would-be adversary has caught your eye," said Whitfield.

"She wagers?" Anthony asked in surprise.

"She'd like to," Leviston answered dryly, "but Bost wouldn't let her join us."

Bost drained his brandy and waved his empty glass at a barmaid. "What do women know about cards? She'll lose her money. Her husband should pay more attention to the purse strings."

Whitfield's eyes glittered. "And if she hasn't got one, she should just say the word. I'd be happy to step in for the night."

Anthony's lips flattened in distaste. "Leave her alone."

"Why?" Bost's laugh was cocky. "You have claims on the lady?"

"*You* certainly do not," Anthony countered icily. His tone served to silence the blackguards.

Good. He needed to keep winning. A brawl over Lady Fortune's honor would have ruined everything.

"Your wine, my lords." The harried barmaid refilled the other gentlemen's glasses, then turned toward Anthony. "Anything for you, sir?"

"Not for me." Anthony placed a gold sovereign he'd set aside onto her tray. "For you. Everyone deserves some good luck once in a while."

Her eyes glistened. "Thank you, sir. *Thank you.*"

Anthony inclined his head. Inn staff would not know him this far north, but he always shared a small token from his winnings. Everyone did deserve good fortune. He couldn't imagine a worse fate than having to be employed to scrape out a living—not only because gentlemen of his class did not work. Anthony had never cleaved to anyone else's schedule or demands. Gaming hells were much more suited to his style of living.

In fact, he won the next several rounds. A thrill shot through him each time. Lady Fortune's presence had made him unconquerable indeed. Tonight's total winnings were well over a hundred pounds.

"I'm out." Bost pushed his chair back and stood

with a disgusted expression. "If I risk any more, I shan't be able to afford to break my fast in the morning."

"Make that two of us." Whitfield glanced at Anthony as he rose to his feet. "I suppose the gossips also lied when they said all the gaming hells in London had closed their doors to you."

"London?" Anthony leaned back in his throne with a careless grin. "Try England. Why do you think I came all the way to Scotland to deprive you of your last ha'penny?"

"Scoundrel." Whitfield shook his head with a chuckle. "Good night, all."

Bost adjusted his hat with a sigh. "Next time I see you, Fairfax, I'm winning back my blunt."

"You can try," Anthony agreed with good cheer before handing the cards to Leviston. "One last round?"

"I'll no doubt regret this," Leviston grumbled as he shuffled the cards.

A movement caught Anthony's eye. He straightened his spine as Lady Fortune rose from her shadowy corner and made her way toward their table. Her very presence dazzled.

"*Now* is there room for a lady?" she asked in a rich, sultry voice.

"Without question." Anthony leaped up in deference while she took her seat. She had no chance of winning, not with Anthony's luck tonight, but he saw no reason not to welcome her to the table.

"Your funeral," Leviston said to her under his breath. "Fairfax here is unbeatable."

Anthony was in full agreement. Leviston could bid his last farthing adieu. Now that Lady Fortune was seated at their table, Anthony's luck would be boundless. He was on the longest winning streak of his life.

"Fairfax, meet Miss Devon." Leviston began to deal the cards. "Starting wager is ten pounds, pet."

She placed her bet on the table without changing expression. Either the sum meant nothing, or she expected to win.

Anthony couldn't stop staring at her from the corner of his eye. He was normally quite gifted at sizing someone up in the briefest of moments—it was the key to reading tables, and knowing when to pass or when to triple his wager—but he couldn't quite get a fix on Miss Devon.

It wasn't just the high-necked modesty of her thick fichu being paired with extravagant rubies, or her concealed golden tendrils and pristine white gloves. Now that she was close enough for him to read her features, he still couldn't do so. Her clear blue eyes were as calm as a winter lake and her pretty, unlined face betrayed nothing.

He was fascinated, tempted to give up on cards altogether in favor of unraveling the far more intriguing mystery beneath the simple, oversized bonnet.

But winning big was his only chance of repaying his debts.

Anthony took the next round, and the round after that. Leviston took the third, only for Anthony to win it back double the following hand with three jacks.

By the fifth round, Leviston's grip on his cards was white-knuckled and he trembled with obvious anxiety.

Miss Devon turned as if to soothe him. "Breathe in through your nose," she murmured, "and out through your mouth. It is but one hand of cards amongst many. A moment in time. Feel your fingers relaxing. If you wish to stop, you may do so. It is only a game."

To Anthony's amazement, Leviston visibly relaxed as he listened to Miss Devon's soft, coaxing words. His knuckles returned to their normal color and his hands ceased trembling.

"You're right," Leviston said with a rueful smile. "How easily we forget that the turn of a card is meaningless overall."

Meaningless? Anthony would have laughed if so much wasn't riding on his continued lucky streak. For him, the turn of the cards meant the difference between eating or not. Between having a roof to sleep under or not. Between being able to look his loved ones in the eyes or consigning them to poverty. Or worse.

Thank God, up 'til now, Lady Fortune had only worked her calming magic on Anthony, or he would not have won a penny. He needed the other players to be on edge. The sight of white knuckles and trembling fingers was his cue to wager big.

Then again, Fate alone dealt the hands. All the subtle cues in the world were useless without the capacity to win.

He glanced down at his cards. Indescribable joy spread through him. He should never have doubted Lady Fortune's effect. A rush of excitement surged through him. Miss Devon could calm Leviston with as many reassuring words as she wished, because Anthony's hand was unstoppable. *Triple aces.* These were truly the best cards he'd ever been dealt in his life. The best cards anyone had ever been dealt.

Leviston was about to go home in tears.

"All in." Anthony dropped the entire contents of his purse next to the pot. "Seventy pounds per player if you stay in."

"Curse you, Fairfax." Color drained from Leviston's face, but he kept a stiff upper lip and ponied up his blunt. "This is my last hand."

With her porcelain face as smooth as a doll's, Miss Devon placed her purse alongside her bet.

A twinge twisted Anthony's stomach. He felt bad about taking money from a lady. It wasn't gentlemanly. Once he won, he would return her portion to her and take the rest straight back to London. The other toffs could afford to lose a few pence, Anthony reasoned, but he needed every penny he could get in order to stay out of prison. Two thousand pounds' worth of pennies, in fact.

It had taken a year of ill luck—and increasingly riskier bets in growing desperation—to amass such mindboggling debt. Because Anthony had always gambled everywhere and with everyone, months had passed before his peers began to realize he had no means to repay them. Not even a few pence. To say they were displeased would be an understatement.

His goal was much higher than repaying his debts, of course. He wanted a pot so full of gold he couldn't budge it without a wheelbarrow. Not only to win enough never to fear being poor again, but also to win big enough so that those he cared about would never lack for anything. He wanted to be *rich*. Not just for a few months or a few years. Forever.

With a sigh, Leviston displayed his cards. A low flush. Poor pup. The man had no chance of winning, and likely knew it.

Anthony felt oddly proud when Lady Fortune turned over her cards to reveal an astonishing hand. Three tens. If Anthony hadn't held triple aces, the mysterious Miss Devon would have swept the table—and the two-hundred-pound pot.

Alas for her, luck was firmly on Anthony's side. This was his night. His streak was invincible. Finally, he could go back home.

He flipped his cards face up with a flourish.

Leviston covered his face with his hat. "I suspected as much."

A streak of visceral, hopeless dismay flashed across Miss Devon's face so quickly that Anthony almost missed it.

"We can play again," he said. "You might earn your money back."

"I'm out," Leviston reminded him with a sigh of regret.

"Not you." Anthony shot him a pointed look. "Miss Devon."

Her eyelashes lowered. "I have no more money."

"You can wager something else." When her blue eyes widened with outrage, he regretted his unfortunate phrasing. Anthony had meant to be gentlemanly, not offensive. He added hastily, "A lock of hair, perhaps. I've just the locket to put it in."

"Don't do it," Leviston advised her under his breath. "This man is why half the members of the House of Lords have grown bald."

Miss Devon's lips twitched. "And yet, I am tempted. What, precisely, is the bet? Just seventy pounds? Or are we playing for the entire pot?"

Anthony stared at her. His blood raced at the idea of such a fearless wager. He should reply "Just seventy pounds" and be done. He *knew* he should. There was nothing to be gained from risking it all. Except for bragging rights when he won the entire pot all over again.

"The whole pot," Anthony assured her magnanimously. She wouldn't win—no one could beat him tonight—but he would still be certain to return her seventy-pound portion to her after he won. This way, she would feel as though she'd had a fair shot.

"Very well." She gave him a brave smile and his insides melted with pride. "I'm in."

As the most impartial party at the table, Leviston agreed to deal again.

Fifteen years of daily gaming was the only reason Anthony's body didn't betray him with even a flicker of satisfaction upon seeing his first card. It wasn't going to be the same hand he'd held last time—that was a rare enough instance he'd dream about for weeks—but it was close enough to steal the breath from his lungs. His luck was damn near unbeatable.

His first card was breathtaking. And the second.

"I'm afraid you won't like my hand," he said when it was time to display triple kings. Twice in a row! What were the chances? His luck was unbreakable.

Leviston nearly choked into his cravat. "How do you *do* it?"

"And I'm afraid you won't like mine," Miss Devon said as she turned over hers.

Anthony froze.

No. She couldn't have triple aces. The only hand capable of beating his.

It was impossible.

A cold sweat broke out on his skin as his stomach dropped… and dropped… and dropped. The room was spinning, spiraling him down into a void of nothingness and despair.

It couldn't be. It just couldn't be.

"I won the entire pot," Miss Devon crowed with delight. She had destroyed him. "Just over two hundred pounds, is it not?"

Anthony stared at her. He wasn't breathing, wasn't blinking. His body wasn't responding to anything his mind offered. How could it? All Anthony could think was *no, no, no.* And, *this is the end.* He needed every florin and crown in his possession in order to keep winning.

How could he possibly have lost it all?

"Y-you can get your pound back from the serving wench," Leviston stammered, clearly suffering just as much shock as Anthony. "A barmaid can't have expected to keep such a sum."

"No," Anthony snapped. "Once I handed over that sovereign, it became hers. The barmaid's luck was in. Mine will have to come back around."

Somehow.

He hoped.

Miss Devon motioned toward the pile of purses

on the table. "May I, then?"

Every muscle in Anthony's body shook with fear and desperation. The night was young. There was plenty more money to be won. Just as soon as he got his winnings back. Or at least a few shillings. Something. *Anything.*

There had to be a way.

Charm, he reminded himself. When his empty wallet got him tossed out through doors, his charm was the one thing that could open new ones.

"Of course," he replied easily, and pushed all three purses to her side of the table as if they contained nothing more valuable than handfuls of dirt. "Although I'm certain you'll return the favor and allow me one last wager, will you not?"

Her expression was more than enough answer. And that answer was no.

"Just enough to stay in the game," he said quickly. "I'm not asking you to wager the full pot. Just give me a chance to win my seventy pounds back. One chance. That's all."

She hesitated, her fingertips mere inches from the stack of full purses. Anthony tried not to fall to his knees and beg.

No, she did not wish to return the favor. Who would? But luck was a powerful seductress, promising lies of invincibility too sweet to resist. Perhaps she would succumb to its sway.

"What would you wager? I'm afraid I don't collect hair," she hedged. "I wouldn't want any of yours."

Relief coursed through Anthony's veins. He had

her. Maybe. He wiggled his eyebrows, affecting a teasing mien. "A boon, that, as I'm quite attached to my mane. Let us wager something far more valuable. If I lose, I'll offer you my… purity."

Her eyes lost their twinkle. "I doubt you have any."

Blast. His ill-advised joke had alienated him even further. Yet there must be *something* a penniless rogue could offer… Anthony leaned back in his chair, careful not to show his desperation. "Then I shall be your slave for the evening. A servant of any sort you desire. I'll darn socks if I have to."

He wouldn't have to, of course. He would win his seventy pounds. And then he would win back the entire pot.

Lady Fortune sent him an arch look as she picked the heavy purses up from the table. "I might enjoy seeing you muck out a chimney."

But she didn't say no.

"Is that a yes?" he asked lightly.

He held his breath as he awaited her decision. Anxiety flooded him. Miss Devon was the most unpredictable card he had ever been dealt. She held all the power. The wisest choice for her would be to leave the cards, pick up the money, and walk away. Then again, gamblers weren't known for making wise decisions.

The question was… What would Miss Devon choose?

Chapter 2

Miss Charlotte Devon hefted the three gaming purses in her hands and hesitated. Should she play another round?

She wasn't penniless. She wasn't even risking the entire pot. She could afford the wager. Besides, her father might even settle a sizable sum upon her, either as a dowry or as an independent living or as…as *something*. Of this, she was certain. The problem was finding him.

In the meantime, she oughtn't to be gambling away fortunes. Even parts of fortunes. The future was too uncertain. She probably ought not to have been gambling at all. But she could do with the money. The other men's earlier rebuff had been so infuriating that when Mr. Fairfax had joined their table and sent her so many curious, amiable glances, the lure had been impossible to resist.

When was the last time a gentleman had sent her a *friendly* look, not a lewd or dismissive one? Come to think of it, when was the last time anyone had been friendly to her at all?

Ladies treated her with disdain, if they even acknowledged her presence. Gentlemen only sought a quick tup with a nameless bit of muslin they could easily discard. As far as society was concerned, Miss Charlotte Devon wasn't a person at all. She was nobody. Meaningless.

Was it any wonder this profligate's roguish smiles and open face had drawn her like a moth to a flame?

It wasn't merely attention from someone above her station. *Everyone* was above her station. Charlotte was long used to being treated as such.

Mr. Fairfax was different. She'd suspected as much from observing his interactions with his peers, yet he continually delighted her. Her surprise when he'd treated the barmaid like a person, rather than a stick of furniture, had turned to amazement when he'd given the woman an entire sovereign to do with as she would. Charlotte's astonishment was eclipsed by shock when he'd lost his winnings and still let the barmaid keep the coin.

His friends had seen nothing wrong with asking for its return. After all, the recipient was a mere serving wench. To them, her sentiments and situation need not enter the equation.

But not to Mr. Fairfax. His gifts were permanent. His debts were his own.

Now he wanted a chance to replay the game. She shouldn't give him one. Perfectly nice gentleman or not. Chimney slave or not. She had won the money fair and square.

But he had given *her* a chance when he should not. When no one else would have done. Charlotte's pulse skipped. No one else had ever cared before. No gentleman, anyway.

He had not only allowed a woman to join his gaming table, but also allowed her to wager nothing more than a lock of hair to stay in the game.

The only explanation for such an illogical act was that Mr. Fairfax was kind to a fault. So how should she repay his kindness?

Undecided, she watched him from beneath her lashes. He might be too handsome and charming for his own good, too reckless and overconfident with his wagers. But, by all appearances, this happy, devil-may-care rogue was also a genuinely nice person.

She would have to return the favor. A begrudging sigh escaped her lips. Blast.

"If you lose, you may escort me safely to the guest quarters," she began, and frowned sternly when he gave his dark eyebrows an exaggerated wiggle. "And then you may return to your own chamber without so much as crossing the threshold into my chamber. Or donating any hair."

His green eyes sparkled at her merrily. "Done."

Laughing in disbelief, Mr. Leviston gathered up the cards and fumbled them into a shuffle. "In case you were unaware, you are both delightfully mad."

Didn't she know it. Charlotte tightened her lips.

She counted seventy pounds back onto the table. "All in?"

"All in." Mr. Fairfax smiled back at her, both dimples showing sweetly.

Charlotte picked up her first card.

If Mr. Fairfax was watching her for a reaction, he would not discern one. Not solely because of Charlotte's legendary self-control. But because she was in shock. Expressionless. Emotionless. Even *she* couldn't believe the hand she'd been dealt.

Three of hearts.

This was surely the worst opening card anyone had ever held in the history of stupid wagers.

She touched her jewels in nervousness. Her necklace and earrings were the sole possessions she could not lose at any cost. She normally wouldn't even wear them in public, but Scotland was the one place where a bit of ostentation might help rather than hurt her cause.

The other reason she wore them was to keep them safe. For the past few days she'd felt as if someone was following her. She never saw the same person two days in a row, but she couldn't shake the uneasy sense of being spied upon.

Today, there had been a man with a limp and a scuffed beaver hat who had stared at her with far more than casual interest. Her breath caught. Perhaps he had seen the jewels and was waiting for her to leave them unattended.

A prickle went down her spine. She was positive the contents of her valise had been rifled through at the last inn. Nothing had been taken—perhaps because the rubies were still on her person. But she couldn't take the risk of losing them.

And now, without her purse, she couldn't even afford to pay a maid or a hall boy to watch over her at night. Just until she was reunited with her father, that was. Protection was the real reason she'd agreed to let accompanying her safely to her chamber be Mr. Fairfax's wager.

That, and she hadn't expected him to win.

She swallowed. No sense drawing out the torture. Stoic, she played all three cards one by one, then lifted her chin. Three of hearts. Three of spades. Five of diamonds. A measly pair. Of *threes*. Charlotte had just lost seventy pounds on the most foolish wager of her life. She glanced up.

Mr. Fairfax was ashen.

Slowly, as if touching his hand was more pain than could be withstood, he displayed his hand.

Nothing. She stared in disbelief.

Ten of spades. King of hearts. Jack of diamonds.

He had *nothing*.

Silence engulfed the table.

She'd won. Charlotte stared at the cards in disbelief. She'd *won*.

Mr. Leviston cackled. "I reckon it's off to clean chimneys for you, Fairfax. Or whatever mischief the two of you decide to get up to."

In a trice, the nameless horror on Mr. Fairfax's face vanished as if it had never existed. His visage resumed the same sunny cheer he had displayed earlier.

He shrugged and clapped Mr. Leviston on the shoulder. "Fortune giveth, and fortune taketh away."

"Every time." Mr. Leviston chuckled. "Shall we have another go tomorrow? I suppose I could scare up a shilling or two."

"You know I've never said no to a game," Mr.

Fairfax replied easily. He fixed his magnetic gaze on Charlotte. "Shall we, my lady?"

As she nodded her acquiescence, her mind was not on the short walk to her chamber, but on how blithely both men shrugged off staggering losses and agreed to repeat the same foolishness the following day.

Were they daft? Charlotte had always supposed town gentlemen could not possibly be as careless and as dissolute as the society papers painted them, but she had clearly been too generous.

Resolute, she rose to her feet. Good. She was glad they were foolish. She could not possibly feel guilty at relieving them of more money than she normally spent in a year if they didn't even have the good sense to miss it. She would be a much better mistress to these purses.

Hope fluttered in her belly. In fact, with two hundred pounds, she could hire a maid before taking the next hack north. She would do so first thing in the morning.

As for tonight… Well. Perhaps fortune truly was on her side.

She slipped her hand about the crook of Mr. Fairfax's arm and let him lead her from the table. With the exception of an off-color jest, he seemed honorable and dignified. With a man like that seeing her safely to her chamber, no scoundrel would dare accost her.

As they exited the common guest area, another gentleman was entering. He pulled up short the moment he laid eyes on them. A chill swept over her as his gaze lingered far longer than necessary.

Please be a friend of Mr. Fairfax, she repeated in her mind. *Please.*

He squinted at her with obvious interest. The wrong kind of interest.

Her stomach sank.

"Do I know you, miss?" His brow furrowed in concentration. "You look incredibly familiar."

"I have one of those faces," she said automatically, and all but hauled Mr. Fairfax out of the common area before the other man could recall where he might have seen a face like hers. Or why Charlotte Devon shouldn't be allowed in the same vicinity as respectable folk.

To his credit, Mr. Fairfax made no protest at being dragged bodily from the room.

As soon as they were safely out of sight, second thoughts immediately crowded Charlotte's brain. The scene was so familiar, she hadn't even questioned it. But what if the man *wasn't* confusing her with her mother? She was in Scotland now. Far from London. What if he hadn't recognized her, but rather her father's rubies? Wasn't that why she'd dropped the assumed name and begun wearing the family jewels the moment she'd crossed the border? Didn't her plan hinge on someone recognizing them and leading her back to her father?

Stupid girl. Her cheeks burned in embarrassment. She was going to have to unlearn two-and-twenty years of rejection and automatic denial if she meant to have success with this mission.

The positive side, however, was that if people were starting to notice a family resemblance, her father must reside in the general area. To be sure, this innkeeper hadn't recognized his name, but someone would—and soon. Her shoulders tensed. If only she knew which it was. Did her mother's famous face carry this far north, or was her father almost within her reach?

"Congratulations on a wonderful win tonight." Mr. Fairfax's warm voice melted over her. "Enviable display of luck."

She looked at him sharply, but his eyes were sincere. "Thank you."

Perhaps he was right. Perhaps fortune was finally on her side. Her heart felt light.

Mr. Fairfax was proof that she was on the right path, the perfect path. The one from where she could start over, find her father, marry a respectable gentleman, and live happily ever after. She straightened her spine.

Finding her father was her only chance to have a good future.

As they neared the dining area, she pointed down a corridor to the right. "My chamber is just up the stairs at the end. If you prefer to leave me here…"

"Nonsense." Mr. Fairfax's green eyes were surprisingly serious. "A wager is a wager. I'll see you safely to your door, and not a step farther."

She nodded, grateful for his presence. It was awful to feel insecure, unsafe. A woman alone was always at risk. One could never truly be *used* to constant unease with one's surroundings, no matter how long one had lived in fear.

Tomorrow would be better. Tomorrow, for the first time since leaving home, she would be able to afford a maid. And the next day, or the day after that, she would have something even better. A *home.*

A sudden buzz of conversation erupted behind them as a crowd of guests exited the dining area together.

Loud footsteps clumped against the wood floor as a man reeking of gin staggered up to them and reached for Charlotte's arm. "I see you found your *dìonadair*, lassie."

Her limbs shook as she froze in fear.

Mr. Fairfax instantly placed himself between Charlotte and the drunkard. "Sir, you overstep. I suggest you find your quarters and stay there."

The crowd from the dining area edged closer to watch.

"Well, you know how it is." The drunkard swayed as he tried to get another look at Charlotte. "With a puss like this looking for a protector, of course a man's going to be interested. When you're done with her—"

Charlotte spluttered. "This man is *not* my 'protector,' nor am I looking for one."

The last thing she needed was for rumors of her supposed easy nature to reach her father's ears. Even *he* wouldn't be able to consider her respectable if she arrived with her reputation as ruined in Scotland as it was in England. But how else could she explain being on Mr. Fairfax's arm, whilst clearly headed toward the guest chambers?

Her mind spun. She needed the crowd to go away. "Mr. Fairfax is just… Mr. Fairfax is my…"

"Husband," he put in smoothly.

"Yes, exactly," she babbled before she could stop herself. That was the perfect excuse. "I am his wife.

We are in a perfectly respectable marital union as husband and wife. Completely reputable and proper."

Splendid. It took all of Charlotte's self-control not to drop her face into her hands at that blurted nonsense. A husband was a better excuse than a lover, but it was also a blatant lie. Mr. Fairfax had only agreed to walk her to her chamber, not to participate in any marital farces along the way. Soon she would be known as a harlot *and* a liar.

The drunkard swayed forward. "Are you sure?"

Charlotte's stomach dropped. Even a drunkard didn't believe such twaddle. She was the least respectable, least proper, least reputable woman in the inn. Any moment now, her name would be just as tarnished here in Scotland as it was back home in London.

To her surprise and relief, Mr. Fairfax didn't so much as change expression.

"Of course I'm certain I'm the lady's husband," he repeated firmly to the drunkard. "Now find your room, or I will put you there myself."

Alarmed, the drunkard scuttled backwards out of harm's way before lurching down the opposite corridor.

Mr. Whitfield stepped up from the rear of the crowd. "Fairfax, you sly dog. No wonder you were making eyes at her all evening. Why didn't you just say that's what you were about?"

Mr. Fairfax met Charlotte's eyes and hesitated.

Her heart pounded. Would he lie to a friend? For her? She held her breath. In her haste to save her reputation, she hadn't considered the ripples she'd be causing in his.

He waved a careless hand in the air. "I'll explain how it all happened next time we see each other at Boodle's. You'll have to buy me a glass of brandy, though. It's quite a story."

Her shoulders sagged with relief. Mr. Fairfax had saved her reputation. He was an angel. Although… how the devil did he expect to get out of this without scandal?

"I expect nothing less than a fantastical tale from you," Mr. Whitfield said with a chuckle. "Boodle's, then."

The last of the crowd dispersed.

Charlotte winced and murmured, "I am so sorry."

"For that twaddle?" Mr. Fairfax turned her away from the crowd and led her down the corridor toward the stairs. "If anything, you've not only guaranteed my readmittance to Boodle's, you even earned me a free glass of brandy while I'm at it. They'll all have a great laugh over the time Anthony Fairfax was married for an entire minute."

Anthony. Charlotte smiled wistfully. He had a lovely name.

Though she would never see him again, she, too, would look back on this moment with fondness. Not because it was a humorous episode or because for one spine-tingling moment she'd been afraid all she'd worked for was about to come crashing down, but because it had been oddly empowering. She'd had no doubt of their ability to fend off a simple drunkard, but convincing a passel of Londoners that a handsome gentleman like him could be married to a nobody like her… She was very, very far from home indeed.

It was magical.

She climbed the wooden stairs with a curve to her lips. The happy smile died when she caught sight of her bedchamber.

The door was ajar.

Her palms went clammy. She gripped Mr. Fairfax's arm. "Someone has been inside my quarters."

"They may still be there." He touched his fingers to her hand. "Stay here and don't move until I ensure it's safe. If you hear any scuffling… scream."

She stared back at him, frozen in place.

He disappeared inside.

She tried to calm her racing heart. Everything was going to be fine. Probably. *Breathe in through the nose, out through the mouth. Imagine muscles relaxing in the neck, the shoulders, the brow.* Mr. Fairfax would be fine. She would be fine.

She stifled a scream when he burst back into view.

Alone.

"No one is inside." He covered her hands with his own. "Do you feel safe in there? Would you like a different chamber?"

Did she feel safe? A bubble of hysterical laughter tangled in her throat. Had she ever truly felt safe?

"It's fine," she managed. She would bar the door and find a maid at first light. "I'm fine."

He studied her for a long moment. "I can stay, if you like."

Fear flashed through her and she shook her head wildly. Not at his offer to watch over her—for a town gentleman, he seemed surprisingly trustworthy—but because if a few steps together in the corridor could raise that many eyebrows, him spending the night in her bedchamber could ruin what little respectability she possessed.

Yet the thought of being left alone was even worse. What if the thief returned to rob her? What if the blackguard wasn't after her money or her jewels, but the unwilling company of a young woman with no one to call out to for help?

"Not inside," Mr. Fairfax said quickly. "I am happy to guard your door from the corridor. You may set as many locks and chairs for barriers as you like. I shan't allow passage to a single soul."

"Y-you would sit in the corridor all night?" Her leaping heart slowed to a more sedate pace at the idea. She hoped his offer was sincere. She already felt safer at the thought of him guarding the threshold from the other side.

"Keeps me from the gaming tables," he answered cheerfully and positioned himself against the wall facing her door.

Relief washed over her. She flashed a grateful smile, but her nerves were still on edge. "Thank you. I would appreciate that."

She appreciated a hall guard more than he could know. But why would he make the offer? Did he truly intend to accede to her every command in order to repay the money he'd lost?

A door creaked open down the hall.

"As my lady wishes." Mr. Fairfax tipped his hat. "I did offer to spend the night doing your bidding. Playing hall boy is certainly less tiring than what I thought you might demand of me. I should be thanking you."

"Shh," she hissed as another door creaked open. "You never thought I was going to ask you for anything. Now mind your tongue. Someone might overhear you."

"But I like granting wishes." His eyes widened innocently. "Have you no desires you'd like fulfilled? I haven't the blunt to buy you a pony—or really anything—but I am quite good with my hands."

"Who's making all that ruckus?" a scratchy voice called out. "Some of us would like to sleep."

Flames of embarrassment shot up Charlotte's cheeks.

Another door swung open and a pale face in a mobcap peered out. "It's Mr. Fairfax holding court in the corridor, by the look of it."

"Holding court?" cackled a voice down the other end of the hall. "Better hope it's with his wife. Had no idea that yellow-haired girl was a married woman. Fairfax ought to keep her close."

"Fairfax ought to keep *quiet*, is what the rotter ought to keep!" bellowed a voice on the other side of the wall. "If that featherwit is still out there chattering to his wife by the time I put my robe on, I'll—"

Charlotte grabbed Mr. Fairfax by the wrist, yanked him into her bedchamber, and slammed the door.

"As I was saying," he began after the briefest pause. "One fine evening, after wagering on races along Rotten Row—"

"Do. Not." She held up a shaking finger and prayed her blush would fade by sunrise. Splendid. She exhaled deeply. Now what? As long as the other guests believed her married to Mr. Fairfax, her reputation was better off with him on the inside of the chamber rather than raising suspicion on the outside. "Don't move an inch until I've had a chance to look about the chamber to see if anything is missing."

His teasing expression faded and his eyes turned serious. "How do you feel?"

"Exasperated," she said through gritted teeth.

"With me." He leaned against the door frame in obvious relief. "Excellent. For a moment there, you looked so pale and terrified that I was afraid to take your arm, for fear you'd shatter." His eyes softened. "I'm glad you're feeling better. You had every right to be alarmed. But the intruder is gone. You are safe. No one will harm you while I guard the door."

Her mouth fell open. Had he made outrageous comments in the corridor to distract her from her panic? Her fingers slowly unclenched as she stared at him. It had worked, blast him. She had gone from shaking with terror to blushing in embarrassment—but she had entered her bedchamber of her own free will. Because she no longer feared it.

"Thank you," she said softly. Although she did not approve of his methods, he had been good to intervene. Her mind had leaped from invasion of privacy to thwarted robbery to the thief returning to ravish her in a matter of moments.

All of those things were everyday threats to a woman of her station traveling alone. It was a relief that, for one night at least, she would not have to lie at the edge of sleep, attuned to every creak of the floorboard and every scratch at her window. Her heartbeat was returning to normal.

To her surprise, she was glad to have Mr. Fairfax with her. He made her feel safe. He made her feel less alone. He made her feel… worth protecting.

The last thing she wanted was for him to know the truth.

She turned away to peruse the chamber in search of damage. It looked the same. Small. Clean. Simple, but remarkably tasteful for such a remote outpost. The wardrobe was open, but she might have left it that way. Perhaps nothing more had occurred than staff forgetting to lock the door after emptying chamber pots and refreshing the water pitcher.

Or Mr. Fairfax might have just saved her from a terrible night, indeed.

She gathered her skirts and the dregs of her serenity. Now that they were stuck together for the night, what was she meant to do with him? Her mother was the one skilled at entertaining gentlemen, not Charlotte. The opposite: she had always done her best not to call untoward attention to herself.

And now she had a man in her bedchamber.

She swallowed. The last thing she wanted was for him to divine her base upbringing. She would simply have to do as she always did, and pretend to be someone else. Someone better than who she really was.

She motioned Mr. Fairfax into the sitting area and settled into a wingback chair near the fireplace with a demure shawl about her shoulders. The role of poor-but-respectable-miss came so readily by now, it was easy to forget she was playacting. Her muscles relaxed. She had spent her entire life trying to be someone she was not. A few more hours wouldn't matter.

Mr. Fairfax strolled close to the fireplace and paused next to the grate. He tossed her an arch look before lifting a poker. "Shall I clean the chimney? I don't at all mind stoking your fire."

She pursed her lips, determined not to let on how much she secretly enjoyed the silly flirtation. Back in London, men didn't bother. They assumed they could have her for a word and tuppence, and even when she rebuked them, they never quite comprehended that she was saving her virginity for something important. Her future.

If she wanted any chance at being respectable one day, at a minimum she needed to keep her maidenhead intact.

It hadn't been easy. Not when her mother earned her living as a courtesan. Keeping house on the first floor, pretending she was no different from any other daughter with a mother who rarely left her bedchamber, had never allowed Charlotte to truly ignore reality. Not when every man who came to the door for her mother's favors offered to buy hers as well.

Twenty years ago, Judith Devon had been one of the most infamous courtesans in all of London. Now, she was simply… old. Forgotten by the fashionable set. Plagued by the lower classes. Her worst enemies—and the only clients she had left.

For the past two-and-twenty years, the only person either of them could count on was each other. Proper ladies and gentlemen treated them like rubbish.

Society never let Charlotte forget her base roots. From the time she was old enough to toddle, gentlemen callers would toss an extra coin her way, and tell her how blessed she was to be the image of her beautiful mother.

It wasn't a blessing. It was a curse.

The mere fifteen-year age gap between them meant, as Charlotte grew older, they were often confused on the street. Pointed at. Spat upon. There was no denying her heritage. No salvaging her reputation. She was a by-blow. A whore's daughter.

Born ruined.

All those long, wretched years, her one chance at some level of respectability was the knowledge that, somewhere out there, she had a father. All she knew about him was his name, that he was a noble laird in Scotland, and that he had no idea he had a daughter.

Her mother had told her he was a wonderful man. Kind, compassionate, wise, thoughtful, gentle—everything a father should be. He hadn't abandoned her. He hadn't even known she existed. He'd returned to Scotland before either of them had realized they'd created a child.

But what if Charlotte could find him?

The tantalizing utopia of living in a respectable household had obsessed her for her entire life. This was her best chance. A man even half as caring and honorable as her mother had painted him would not hesitate to take her in, to welcome her. She didn't want his money. She simply wanted his time. His affection. A place in this world.

As a child, Charlotte had lain awake every night dreaming about the day he would discover her and whisk her away to a better life, far from London. For years, she'd actually believed her father would return to rescue both her and her mother.

He never had. So here she was. An adult now. Closer to her dream than she'd ever been. He would not sweep in to save her, so Charlotte would have to do so herself. First, she had to find him—convince him she was virtuous enough to take in.

Then she would persuade him to send for her mother, or at least provide for her. Every new client Mother was forced to take added lines to her face and took years from her life. Charlotte was determined to marry well and rescue her mother herself, if her father could not. But to do so, she had to portray herself as honorable and proper.

Starting with never admitting to the truth.

"That should do it." Mr. Fairfax slid the fire iron back into its stand and turned from the grate. "What is my next chore?"

Charlotte gazed up at him, startled. She had thought the farce was over. "You truly wish to be my slave for the night?"

"Of course I don't *wish* to," he assured her. "But I wouldn't want it said that I reneged on our wager. Now, what shall it be? I likely oughtn't to divulge a secret, but I am world renowned for a quite unparalleled foot massage."

She frowned repressively. "If it's a secret, how are you world renowned?"

"I'm also not half bad at dressing hair and mending hems," he continued without pause. "I minded my younger sister and often had to play maid-of-all-work when times were lean." He lowered his voice. "Playing maid-of-all-work is not nearly as diverting as playing whist or Faro, but a boy of twelve does not sail his own ship."

Try as she might, Charlotte couldn't keep a smile from forming. What must it be like to grow up so secure in one's self-worth that one could admit to such poverty and have the confession sound charming? Either she truly did not understand the ton, or Mr. Fairfax wasn't as well-connected as it had seemed in the common room.

Then again, he was welcome at fashionable gentlemen's clubs like Boodle's. So which was it?

She narrowed her eyes. "Do you know any dukes or earls?"

"I know scads of dukes and earls," he assured her. "However, most are married and the rest are scandalous, so I really cannot recommend them to a lady."

"Name one," she challenged.

"The Duke of Ravenwood," he answered immediately. "First-rate fellow, married to an absolutely dreadful hoyden who I love quite dearly. Cannot recommend her, either. Bad for one's reputation."

Charlotte tilted her head, unsure whether to believe even half of his tales. "Name a scandalous lord."

"Lord Wainwright," he said without hesitation. He lowered his voice. "The majority of his interactions with society are horizontal. A frequent guest at the even more scandalous Duke of Lambley's infamous masquerade balls."

She crossed her arms. Both of those names often appeared in the scandal sheets. Which did not mean Mr. Fairfax knew either gentleman personally. "Are any of these rakes and do-gooders as skilled as you at darning socks?"

"You know, I've never asked them," he said with wide-eyed innocence. "I shall add it to my diary straightaway, so as not to forget the next time we meet."

She harrumphed to hide her amusement. It didn't matter whether he knew the men. She would never be introduced to them. "How are you at pressing wrinkles from gowns?"

"Let me assure you," he said with utter seriousness, "that I have never worn a wrinkled gown in all my life."

"Very gentlemanly." She tried not to smile. "Let's see your skill as maid-of-all-work, then. My gowns are in the wardrobe, as is my traveling iron. See what you can do."

"At your service." He bowed, then turned and marched to the wardrobe like a soldier off to war.

Now that he couldn't see her, she let herself grin. The man was incorrigible… but she couldn't help but find his frankness humanizing and his silliness refreshing. "You're certain you know what you're about with those gowns?"

"You will think my valet pressed them," he called back in a tone filled with such portent that Charlotte half expected her muslins to be dotted with burns in the shape of smoothing irons.

It would almost be worth it, just to have this one night. This memory of a man above her station treating her as if she were above his. Of being an equal, rather than an object incapable of feelings or rights of her own. Of feeling… happy. She hugged herself in astonishment. When was the last time she'd felt safe enough and carefree enough to be *happy*?

She gazed wistfully at his strong back as he placed the iron in the fire. He smoothed out the first gown on the chaise longue before dampening the wrinkled material with water from the pitcher.

A man like this was even more dangerous than the sort who usually approached her, she realized in surprise. A man like this wouldn't just take what he wanted. He'd make her want to give it to him of her own free will. Desire him. Long for his kisses. Plead for more.

She forced herself to look away.

No. She would *not* be like her mother. She had promised herself that the first time she'd seen her mother cry. Charlotte's life would be different. She'd find a way to be respectable if it killed her.

Which meant keeping her distance from the tempting Mr. Fairfax. No matter what happened.

Charlotte still had dreams for the future. She'd sworn to never so much as kiss a man, much less lie with him, until she was in love. She would only give herself once, to the right man. The gentlemen she'd wed would be perfect. Some handsome, moneyed, landed, laird friend of her father's.

Or at the very least, her husband would be above reproach. And very much in love. The rest was optional… but a girl could dream.

A knock sounded upon the door. "Miss Devon? It's Mr. Garman, the innkeeper."

Frowning, she pushed herself out of the wingback

chair. What could the innkeeper want at this hour?

When she opened the door, his expression was apologetic. "I'm so sorry to bother you, miss, but I must inquire… Is Mr. Fairfax within this chamber?"

"I'm busy ironing my lady's morning gown," Mr. Fairfax called from somewhere behind Charlotte's shoulder. "'Tis ever so relaxing!"

She pasted on a pained smile. "He's here."

"And, pardon me asking, miss, but it's a matter of some importance. Is Mr. Fairfax your husband?"

Charlotte's throat dried. It had been one thing to playact in the corridor, but now that the gentleman in question was otherwise unaccompanied inside her bedchamber…

Her fingers grew cold. Scotland didn't know her past. If she wanted to keep her reputation, there was only one possible answer. She just didn't dare give it. One lie was enough. She wouldn't involve Mr. Fairfax any more than she already had.

"Yes," he called from somewhere near the fireplace. "Of course the lady is my wife. Do you think I extend my ironing services to all your guests?"

"Yes," she echoed faintly, forcing herself not to clap her hands with relief. "I'm afraid Mr. Fairfax is indeed my husband."

The innkeeper yanked a very expensive, very battered valise from the hallway to her open doorway. He lifted his chin to project his voice over Charlotte's shoulder. "In that case, these are the items we are certain your husband *accidentally* left behind in the bedchamber he *forgot to pay for* in the excitement of reuniting with his wife. I assume he'll be down *first thing in the morning* to settle the bill?"

"Absolutely, tomorrow," Charlotte's faux husband called back. "I have a whist appointment with Leviston after noon, and then I'll settle everyone's bills. I can feel my luck upon the wind!"

Several doors along the corridor cracked ajar, and various occupants peeked out, their gazes shamelessly curious.

The innkeeper cut Charlotte a flat look. "Given your husband's reputation for forgetfulness in monetary matters, would you be so kind as to remind him tomorrow of his promise?"

"We'll pay you right now," she said quickly, lowering her voice to a whisper so the onlookers could not overhear. "What's the balance, including a full day's meals?"

She counted out the sum from her winnings and sent the innkeeper on his way before every head under this roof was pointed in her direction. Her hands shook. She despised being the subject of gossip. She could not remain a guest here a moment longer than necessary.

Tomorrow morning, she would leave at dawn and put as much distance between herself and Mr. Fairfax as humanly possible. He was charming, but apparently not as upper crust as she had presumed. She could not chance becoming an object of ridicule in Scotland, too. Had he only offered to save her because he required saving, himself?

That was the only answer. *Blackguard.* Once the door was shut and locked, she turned back toward the fireplace.

"You offered yourself as maid-of-all-work because you couldn't afford to stay through the night," she accused.

"I offered to fulfill the lady's every desire," he corrected with a playful wink. "You were the one who preferred I employ my talented fingers with an iron."

She glared at him. But her true disappointment was in herself. Of course a dapper gentleman would not offer himself as hall boy—much less chambermaid—out of the goodness of his heart. If she hadn't been so frightened by the break-in, such improbable charity would have raised every suspicion.

He blinked innocently. "I should mention that I am happy at any time to cease ironing and go back to the original plan of—"

"That was never my plan," she bit out. Yet she could not summon true anger. Regardless of his motives, he had saved her from ruining her reputation, and was watching over her to keep her safe lest the thief return in the night. As to his manner of offering it… Undoubtedly her low upbringing caused her to find his irreverence more charming than scandalous. But she could not let it show. "I have no interest in participating in misconduct of any kind. Come morning, we shall part ways as strangers."

"Yes, my lady. Your indifference is quite clear." He returned the iron to the fire and held up the first gown. "How am I doing with this one?"

She stalked forward, intending to yank it out of his hands—then stopped short when she realized the condition of the gown was absolutely impeccable. No wrinkles. No burn marks. Just soft, warm muslin.

"It'll do," she said grudgingly.

His smile was angelic. "Allow me to fold it and place it in your valise in such a way that when you arrive at your next destination it will be just as perfect as it is at this moment."

She no longer doubted that he could do it. Nor could she deny that his offers of help were both competent and sincere. Her shoulders relaxed. Perhaps his hardworking upbringing had made him more of a gentleman, not less of one.

"I hope you're not expecting to sleep, maid-of-all-work." She returned to the wingback chair and rested her tired head against the side. "I have plans for you all night long."

"Those are my favorite kinds of plans," he assured her. "Ask anyone."

She raised an eyebrow in stony silence. She couldn't allow him to guess that she was far more intrigued than offended.

For all that her mother's paramours had declined in attractiveness and wealth over the years, her mother had truly seemed to enjoy the company of a few favorites.

Being forced to spend a night trapped in a bedchamber with a charming, talented rake was far from a nightmare. No one with a pulse could blame a lonely young lady for being tempted to make some very bad decisions with a man as handsome as Mr. Fairfax.

But carnal relations were a dark road, and Charlotte would not let herself travel down that path.

"Traditional nocturnal activities are slightly different," he acknowledged. "That is your fault, I might point out. You should take this moment to think about your actions and the importance of better decision making. I will be happy to meet you again tomorrow at the gaming table so you can attempt to correct this devastating mistake."

She tried not to smile. Or to show the inner war playing out between her brain and her desire. "You can't fool me. All you want is to win the money back."

His eyes widened. "Not *all* I want. If an unfortunate turn of the cards were to force me to share your bed, I should have to do the gentlemanly thing and follow through. Luckily for both of us, rumor has it I'm even better at certain entertainments than I am at pressing gowns."

Her cheeks heated at the idea of finding out just how talented he might be. She gave him a scolding look. "I'm afraid we shall not have an opportunity to find out. I'll be leaving at first light. I doubt we will meet again."

"Ah, such is Fate." His tone was light, but his eyes looked genuinely sorry to see her go. "At least we'll always have… Where are we?"

She curled into the wingback chair. "Oxkirk."

"Oxkirk. Of course. My new favorite town." He tilted his head. "Thus far, you are definitely my favorite thing about Scotland."

"Thus far?" She gave him a mock frown. "How temporary. Will you have a new wife tomorrow?"

"You shall not be present," he answered primly, "and thus you needn't be jealous."

Needn't be, perhaps. Charlotte looked away. She liked the idea of him charming the chemise off some proper debutante much less than she ought.

She pulled a blanket over her shoulders and snuggled into the oversized chair to watch him iron. Or perhaps to admire his shoulders. And the way the firelight lit his chestnut hair with glints of gold.

Her heavy eyelids were almost completely closed when he finished the last of her gowns.

Without bothering her, he sat down to tug off his boots and ready himself for sleep.

Concern for her reputation ripped through her drowsiness. Quickly, she scrambled out of the chair and onto the four-poster bed so that she would not be in the vicinity of a gentleman in his stocking feet.

She closed the bed curtains as best she could, but a gap between the cloth panels gave her a clear view of Mr. Fairfax removing his cravat and folding it neatly.

He blew out the last candles. "Go to sleep and dream about what might have been."

Charlotte did not dare respond.

She watched through her eyelashes as his silhouette stripped off its tailcoat and waistcoat and stretched out on the chaise longue before the low fire. Her heart pounded. He was now wearing merely breeches and a linen undershirt.

A proper young lady with a respectable upbringing would likely require smelling salts to recover from such a scandalous predicament. Charlotte, however, fought a traitorous thrill at being so close to forbidden fruit. She could not help but remember his words.

"Are you going to dream about what might have been?" she asked him softly, emboldened by the darkness.

His reply was almost too soft to hear. “Possibly forever.”

Chapter 3

Anthony was just finishing his morning shave to the sound of roosters and whinnying horses when a creak of the mattress indicated that Miss Devon had awakened as well.

"Good morning, my love," he called out as he rinsed his straight razor in a small basin. "You'll be appalled to know this chaise longue isn't fit for a pig to sleep upon. I never quite got used to my legs dangling off the end, and my neck is so stiff I won't be able to turn my head to the left for days."

"Why would a pig stay in a bedchamber?" She swung her legs off the mattress and rubbed her face. "And what ungodly hour is it?"

"Six," he answered brightly.

"*Six?*" She groaned in dismay. "I would've thought a prodigal rake might be counted upon to sleep until at least ten."

"And that is what you get for assuming all prodigal

rakes act in precisely the same way. Let that be a lesson to you." He shook a finger at her.

She fell back against the mattress with a moan. "Why on earth are you awake?"

"Hmm, I'm not sure," he said. "Did you miss the part about my legs dangling into the abyss all night or the bit about my neck bones being fused at an odd angle? The next time we share a room, I'm taking the bed."

"Then where do *I* sleep?" she asked tartly.

"Also the bed." He turned back to the looking glass to dry his face. "Do try to pay attention."

"Do try to stop dreaming." Although she was still lying back with her eyes facing the tester, a telltale smile played at the edges of her lips.

Pleasure warmed him. He slipped his razor into his valise and curled his fingers about the handle. "I'm afraid I'm utterly presentable, and cannot prolong my morning toilette for a moment without putting shame to Brummell himself. If you like, however, I could stay just long enough to accompany you to breakfast?"

"To my chagrin, I would like that very much." She sat up, her expression now serious. "But I've dallied longer than I should, and must be off immediately."

He bowed and picked up his valise. "Perhaps I'll see you one day in London?"

She shook her head. "I'm afraid that's the last place we'd cross paths. Perhaps we'll see each other again someday in Scotland." A smile tugged at her lips. "So far, you've been my favorite husband."

"So far?" he teased, echoing her earlier mock outrage. "Shall you replace me so easily?"

She grinned back at him. "You needn't be jealous. We'll always have… where are we again?"

"The Kitty and Cock Inn," Anthony replied, straight-faced. If he were to be honest, he'd chosen the inn largely because of its name.

"The Kitty and Cock Inn. Has there ever been a more romantic posting house?" She clutched her hands to her heart as if tempted to swoon. "Good luck at the gaming tables, Mr. Fairfax. May fortune be with you."

"It already is. Farewell, my lady." He strode out of the chamber and into the corridor, and shut the door smartly behind him before he could do anything so foolish as dare to kiss her goodbye.

If she had let him, he might not have wished to stop.

What if she would not have wished to stop, either?

Anthony hurried toward the stairs before he could continue this line of thought. Much as he liked Miss Devon, a man as penniless as he was in no position to take on an idle flirtation. He couldn't afford a wife, much less a mistress.

That the innkeeper had believed the claim was testament to just how far he was from home.

He shook his head as he entered the stairwell. Thank God no one who knew him would ever believe the rumors, should gossip about their Scottish encounter ever reach London. The last thing he needed was to embroil himself in a compromise, no matter how much he'd liked Miss Devon.

If he'd had the blunt, he would have loved to have

at least been able to treat her to grander accommodation. A luxurious suite of her own. Which she would perhaps invite him to share…

Enough mooning. He rolled his shoulders. He had games to play and money to win. Someone would surely seed him a shilling, and by this time tonight his troubles might be nearly over.

He strode out into the corridor. His stomach rumbled. Unlike last night, at this hour few guests milled about the inn's common areas. But the kitchen would undoubtedly be open. And his temporary wife had already paid for the day's meals.

A pang of self-loathing made his muscles tense. *He* should be the one paying for meals. A better gentleman would've had the blunt to hire Miss Devon a maid, rather than resort to doing the honors himself. Hadn't he sworn to never again pick up an iron?

Anthony's shoulders sagged. How he wished he hadn't been blown up at Point Non Plus. Money was happiness. When he was flush, life was perfect. He could make all his friends and family happy. Buy them anything they wished. Be wanted. When times were tight, the only doors that opened to him were those of the debtors' prison.

He pushed the negative thoughts away as he set down his valise by the entrance to the dining room.

Enough. His luck always managed to turn around. No matter how dire things became, if he believed in himself and kept wagering ever higher, fortune eventually found him. Had he not recovered from similar losses dozens of times before?

Today would be more profitable. He would even

have breakfast! More importantly, he'd spent the entire night in the presence of Lady Fortune herself. How could he possibly lose?

"Well, if it isn't Mr. Fairfax," came a rough voice from behind his shoulder.

Anthony whirled about.

Two burly, hulking ruffians with cold eyes and scarred faces had him cornered with his back to a wall. One of the men had mean fists and bloodshot eyes. The other had a hard smile and pockmarks covering his face.

"What can I do for you gentlemen?" Anthony asked as if their presence incited no concern whatsoever. *Charm*, he reminded himself. 'Twas the one currency he couldn't lose at a gaming table. "Care to join me for eggs and kippers?"

"Care to pay your vowels?" snarled the one covered in pockmarks.

Anthony forced a carefree grin. His IOUs had been legendary but scattered until the owner of a vice parlor had purchased them. Previously, Anthony and the tempestuous Maxwell Gideon had been friends. He was unsurprised to learn now they were not. That was how money worked. Or rather, the lack thereof.

"Tell Gideon I'll have part of it tonight. I've an appointment at the tables and I—"

"Won't tell him nothing." Pockmarks cracked his knuckles. "You'll give us the goods directly, or we hog-tie you straight to Marshalsea."

Anthony swallowed. Gideon didn't just possess Anthony's IOUs. To keep what was left of their friendship—and to buy more time—Anthony had signed an actual contract promising to repay the debt. A promise he had yet to keep, despite his continual efforts. The sums were no longer mere debts of honor, but legally actionable. A chill shivered down his spine.

There was no money to give. Once he was locked in debtors' prison, he would never be set free.

His shoulders straightened in determination. He needed to try a different tack. Appeal to the ruffians' logic.

"If I rot in Marshalsea, how will Gideon ever get his blunt?" he asked.

"From your wife," Pockmarks replied instantly.

"My what?" Anthony almost burst out laughing. "Gideon knows I don't have a wife."

"Of course you do." Pockmarks smirked. "We heard you say so."

Everyone did, by the sound of it. Anthony shook his head, his smile fading. A niggle of worry slid down his spine. He had meant to disperse the crowd, not cause more trouble. "I swear it meant nothing. Just a bit of playacting. We aren't married."

"That's where you're wrong." The other ruffian's smile showed broken teeth. "This is Scotland. Once you say it, it's true."

"You mean… *legally?*" Anthony stammered in disbelief at such an absurd practice. His stomach bottomed in dread.

God's teeth. He'd known Scots law allowed for irregular marriages, but one would think they'd at least require a priest or a few witnesses. His blood ran cold. There had been plenty of witnesses. If saying he was married made it true, there would be no way to deny it.

And now Miss Devon was caught in Anthony's mess.

"Can I annul just by saying so, too?" Desperation clawed through him. "I am no longer married. She is not my wife. Leave her out of this."

"You can't undo anything without involving the courts." Pockmarks stepped closer.

Broken Tooth licked his lips. "Did you consummate?"

"No," Anthony blurted in relief, never so happy to have behaved like a gentleman.

"Doesn't matter." Broken Tooth smirked. "She's yours."

Pockmarks flexed his fingers. "Which means them jewels she was wearing… are ours."

No. Anthony's heart raced in horror. He could not let his past debts involve Miss Devon, much less strip her of her possessions. She was innocent. This disaster was Anthony's, and his alone.

But was it, legally? His breath grew shallow. By marriage, anything a wife possessed became her husband's property. And anything Anthony possessed… belonged to Maxwell Gideon. His blood chilled.

The ruffians were right. Either he surrendered items he had no business touching, or these blackguards had every right to drag him bodily to prison. At the very least, he needed time to undo his inadvertent marriage.

"I need three months," he said as authoritatively as he could. These ruffians might be hired muscle for a gaming hell, but Anthony moved in society. Perhaps their class difference could buy him a little time. "Her jewelry isn't worth a fraction of what I owe. In three months, I'll hand Gideon the entirety. In person."

"You don't get three months." Broken Tooth crossed his arms over his large chest.

"Two," Anthony suggested quickly. "With an extra five percent for yourselves. I promise."

Broken Teeth exchanged a glance with his partner. "We'll give you a fortnight."

Pockmarks flicked a speck of dust from Anthony's waistcoat. "And not a minute more."

His breath hitched in panic. Impossible. Two weeks wasn't long enough to win back enough funds to repay all his debts. His limbs shook. "Then no bonus for you. It can't be done. I need to pay in installments. I need time. Ten percent a fortnight from now, then ten percent every week until the debt is paid in full."

"No installments," Pockmarks snarled. "We've already given you time. If you don't want gaol fever, you'll settle your debts two weeks from today."

"And if you don't pay in full…" Broken Tooth's smile was terrifying. "You'll hand over everything you and your wife own, and *still* go to prison."

"Don't forget…" Pockmarks tipped his hat. "We'll be watching."

Chapter 4

Charlotte washed and dressed with renewed confidence. As unexpectedly wistful as she'd felt upon realizing she'd never see Mr. Fairfax again, her life balanced on the precipice of a huge, positive change. With luck, today was the day she'd meet Laird Dìonadair, her father.

Or at least find out where he lived.

She fastened her jeweled earrings to her ears, then concealed the matching necklace in one of the pouches strapped beneath her bound breasts. The bandages had always been the most important part of her wardrobe.

Years ago, she'd started hiding her curves to disguise her resemblance to her mother, but the tight band of linen had quickly become a convenient place to hide objects of value she didn't wish to be stolen. Particularly along the weather-beaten cobblestone alley where she had grown up, or on the crowded mail coach she'd taken to leave London forever.

Here in Scotland, however, wearing the rubies was a necessary risk. It was the only way to gain the laird's attention.

Because he'd left before she was born, Charlotte wouldn't be able to recognize her father even if they ran into each other on the street. He and his relatives, on the other hand, would immediately recognize family jewels. The rubies were the key to success.

Her father would recognize them as the jewels he'd gifted to Charlotte's mother. By which he would recognize Charlotte herself, and immediately invite her to be part of his family.

She hoped.

All she wanted was to be someone who mattered. She didn't need the laird's money. Not if she could have his love. Or at least his acceptance.

Her father was not just a laird. Everything her mother had ever told her indicated he was a kind and honorable man who always did the right thing. It wasn't his fault he was never told of Charlotte's birth. Once they met, he would embrace her and exclaim over her and proclaim himself proud to have a daughter. He was that kind of man. She sucked in a shaky, hopeful breath.

She was mere days or even hours away from meeting her respectable father. From being *welcomed* somewhere. From being launched as a valued member of real society. Gone were the years of being shunned and looked down upon. She would be someone else at last. Someone accepted without question. Perhaps even loved. The thought of becoming part of his family made her dizzy with joy. Her childhood dreams were finally close enough to touch.

Thanks to Mr. Fairfax, Charlotte's gowns were perfectly ironed and already tucked neatly away in her trunk. She placed a few final toiletries on top and closed the lid with determination. The day was beautiful. Perhaps even perfect. She would find a maid, find a coach, and then find her father.

A sudden knock rattled the chamber door.

She frowned. The innkeeper's knock hadn't sounded so frantic last night, when the older man hadn't known if his debts would be paid. What on earth could he want now? She opened the door.

To her surprise, the wild-eyed man in the corridor was not the innkeeper at all, but Mr. Fairfax.

"Apologies," he said as he swung his valise into the chamber and secured the lock. "You must let me in."

She blinked in confusion. "I was just leaving, I'm afraid. If you'll be so kind as to help me with my trunk, you may stay in the room until noon. The account is paid." She smiled up at him. "How was breakfast?"

"Miss Devon." He scrubbed his face with his hands, then grabbed her shoulders. "No. Not Miss Devon. Mrs. Fairfax. May God forgive me."

She laughed. "I think we can dispense with that fiction now. Once we both go our separate ways, there's no reason for—"

"We're married." His fingers were tight, his eyes glassy with panic. "Look at me. We're *married*."

Her smile faded. "What in heaven's name are you nattering on about?"

He released her and fell back against the wainscoting, his face full of misery. "Scots law. I'm talking about Scots law. If two people affirm aloud that they are married to the other, that act legally has the same weight as marriage in a church, after banns and before God."

"It… What?" Her stomach dropped. "We c-can't be married."

He rubbed his forehead. "I didn't trust the source either, so I awakened Leviston, who confirmed my fears. Even had the stones to offer me an extra round of drinks at Boodle's to celebrate, the rotter."

She staggered backwards in growing horror. "No. This can't be happening."

He grimaced. "You have no idea."

Her lungs gasped for air as if she were drowning. She clutched her chest. Impossible. How could she be married to a total stranger? All the joy seeped from her limbs.

There went her dreams of marrying someone who loved her. Who *wanted* her. Who could have had his pick of women, but whose heart belonged solely to her. Who knew her inside and out, and was not ashamed to claim her as his own.

Her hands trembled. Fear clawed through her. How could this possibly be true?

"We need to speak with a barrister." She hugged herself. "Immediately."

Mr. Fairfax ran a hand through his hair. "We're in Scotland. I don't know any barristers. If we were in London…"

"If we were in London, we wouldn't even need to

have this conversation. Come." She motioned him out of her chambers and into the corridor, then turned to lock the door behind them. "I do know a barrister. I met his wife earlier this week."

Mrs. Oldfield had been asking the ladies in the common salon whether they thought book clubs or sewing circles to be more prestigious. Charlotte had declined to opine on the more meritorious, and instead offered suggestions on how to improve attendance and engage interest with either style. Mrs. Oldfield proclaimed Charlotte the most level-headed young woman of her acquaintance, and had invited her to tea that very afternoon, as if Charlotte were an actual lady of equal standing.

And now Charlotte would have to confess to Mrs. Oldfield's husband that she'd accidentally handfasted herself to a perfect stranger. Mortification heated Charlotte's cheeks. Shoulders tight, she turned and strode toward the stairs.

When she and Mr. Fairfax reached the common area, neither of the Oldfields were present. Charlotte had the innkeeper send a footman with a note requesting an audience with Mr. Oldfield, then settled down to wait at a small table with Mr. Fairfax. She clasped her hands to hide their tremble.

Up until today, the inn's common salon had been home to some of Charlotte's best memories in recent history. The further she journeyed from London, the less likely other travelers were to guess she wasn't the respectable miss she pretended to be. For almost a week, she had spent delightful afternoons in this very room, chatting with the other women over tea, and developing a small reputation as a fine sounding board for ladies seeking advice.

And now, the only advice that mattered was whatever Mr. Oldfield suggested to get them out of this dreadful pickle. Charlotte hadn't intended ever to see Mr. Fairfax again, much less marry him. As soon as they undid the damage, the better.

His green eyes were beseeching. "Miss Devon, when I claimed we were married, I was only trying to help. A crowd had formed, and making them believe there was nothing remarkable to see was the fastest way to disperse them."

"I know why you did it." She twisted her earring nervously. "I thought the same thing you did. It's why I went along."

"I never thought it would mean…" Mr. Fairfax blew out a slow breath.

Charlotte closed her eyes. Of course he hadn't thought a meaningless lie would legally bind him to a total stranger. What reasonable person would? She opened her eyes. This was a disaster.

Married. No worse farce could have befallen them. Who was this man? Would he want *her*?

Certainly not once he knew the truth. And then what would that leave them?

"Listen." Mr. Fairfax hesitated, then took her hands in his. "The situation is more complicated than you know."

"More complicated than us being married?" she said bleakly. God save them both.

"Vastly." His visage was pale. "It's one thing to be

penniless…"

She swallowed the sour taste in her throat. Penniless. The thought terrified her. As her mother's youth and beauty had dried up—and as Charlotte's resolve not to follow in her footsteps had grown—their once-comfortable home had become old and shabby. But they had never been penniless. The townhouse was paid for, and her mother had saved enough in Campbell and Coutts to ensure she and her daughter would at least have bread and firewood for the rest of her life. But it hadn't come to that.

Her mother's days of fireworks and theatre might be long gone, but Charlotte had never lacked for food and clothing. The house might be worn at the edges, but Charlotte had always been presentable. It hadn't been enough, of course. Even if she were wearing her nicest gown, every nose turned up whenever she walked by.

Somehow, people knew she wasn't good enough.

On good days, they wouldn't belittle her into tears. On bad days… Well. She certainly knew what it was like to have doors slammed in her face. The world was huge, but mostly consisted of places a whore's bastard daughter was not allowed to go.

Yet, she'd never been beggared.

"It's one thing to be penniless," Mr. Fairfax repeated, appearing to gather strength. "But my situation is significantly worse. An improbable run of poor fortune struck me at the gaming tables, and I now owe two thousand pounds I cannot begin to repay."

Horror filled her. *Two thousand pounds?* An unattainable sum. They were ruined before they'd even begun.

Worse, if Mr. Fairfax could not fulfill his debts of honor, he was no gentleman at all.

She yanked her hands from his and took a step backwards. Their union had done the impossible and made her status even *worse.*

Ruined. Her dreams of marrying into a respectable family gone forever. A husband she didn't want. Debts she could not afford.

He'd wrecked both their lives.

"You can have your winnings back," she said, her voice bleak. To her, last night's windfall of two *hundred* pounds had been a staggering sum to win at the gaming tables. For him to owe ten times as much money… How many games must he have lost? "Two thousand pounds… I'm afraid I don't have that kind of resources."

"I know you don't," he said, his tone earnest. "I wouldn't ask it of you even if you did. Nor do I want your purse or anything else of yours."

"You should take last night's winnings," she said with a sigh. She hadn't expected to play, much less win that much. She should have stayed focused on finding her father. "That two hundred pounds would have been yours if you hadn't let me back in the game."

"I cannot." Mr. Fairfax ran a hand through his hair and took a deep breath. "My debts are mine, not yours."

"If this marriage stands, the debts will be ours. At least take your own purse," she insisted, still unable to believe this was happening. "I won't be able to use it without feeling as though every penny I spend is consigning you to prison."

"Fine. But keep your own purse. It doesn't belong to me."

A shadow fell across the table.

"Good morning, Mr. Oldfield," Charlotte said warmly. "Please, take a seat. This gentleman and I have a quick legal concern we'd like to talk over with you."

"A legal concern, is it?" The barrister took the seat opposite Charlotte. "In that case, I shall have to charge for my professional advice. Ten pounds should do."

"Ten—" Mr. Fairfax choked, his face empurpling. No doubt he considered the loss of each pound note would only dig his grave ever deeper.

"Here." She peeled the notes from her own purse and slid them across the table. No matter what fee the barrister charged, they had to understand their predicament—and how to stop it.

Mr. Oldfield pocketed the banknotes. "Very well, then. How may I help you?"

"Are you familiar with Scots law?" Mr. Fairfax asked. "Specifically, the laws governing irregular marriages?"

Mr. Oldfield's startled gaze flew from Mr. Fairfax's wan countenance to Charlotte's. "Oh, dear."

She nodded. "I'm afraid so. Please tell me it isn't so."

The barrister leaned forward. "What, precisely, has happened? Tell me the exact wording you used."

Mr. Fairfax grimaced. "I repeatedly said, 'I am her husband' in front of about a dozen witnesses."

Mr. Oldfield raised his brows toward Charlotte.

"And I said, 'I am his wife.' In front of the same witnesses."

It had seemed so clever at the time. A tiny lie so forgettable, she'd given it no further thought once she was back in her guest chamber.

A lie poised to ruin her life.

"In that case…" The barrister leaned back in his seat. "I'm afraid you've made a binding contract. You are indeed married."

"*What?*" Charlotte's blood ran cold. It couldn't be!

Mr. Fairfax looked as if he might swoon right out of his chair. "How? Why?"

The barrister folded his hands. "That section of Scots law was enacted to protect innocents from those who would take advantage of them. Scotland has many remote villages without means for a traditional marriage. A perfect breeding ground for unscrupulous curs who like to prey on girls, by assuring naive maidens they'll be properly wed at the first opportunity—only to disappear from town as soon as they've divested her of her purity."

"It's a law to protect women." Charlotte gritted her teeth at the irony. "And it's trapped us in an unwanted marriage."

Mr. Oldfield inclined his head. "The law has done wonders to save innocent virgins from ruin. If a man claims his intention is to wed her, the couple need only announce their union before witnesses for it to be legal from that moment forward. It's also known as the Law of Mutual Agreement."

"Not *well* known," Mr. Fairfax muttered. "I certainly had no idea what I was getting into."

"Is there nothing that can be done?" Charlotte asked the barrister. "Can we not simply pretend it never occurred? By mutual agreement?"

Mr. Oldfield frowned. "The two of you are technically and legally married. That said, if those who witnessed you publicly presenting yourselves as married are strangers whom you are unlikely to ever see again, and who have no knowledge of your names…" He hesitated. "I cannot *advise* you to lie about a legally binding marriage, because any future union would be bigamy, not to mention the property laws governing married couples. But if there is truly no chance of the incident ever being mentioned again—"

"Thank you ever so much," Charlotte gushed as hope filled her once more. "That is exactly what we—"

"—are not in a position to do," Mr. Fairfax finished grimly. His countenance had drained of all color.

"Why ever not?" she demanded, as panic once more slid across her skin.

He pushed his hair from his wan brow. "You may recall that I owe quite a bit of money to a powerful man?"

Her stomach dropped. "He's *here?*"

"Not him. The ruffians he sent to fetch his blunt from me by force."

"They threatened you?"

"They tried to. I managed to buy an extra fortnight before the debt comes due." He met her gaze. "But they witnessed our ill-fated announcement. It's ironclad."

Ironclad. A cursed leg-shackle binding her to a man who gambled as if he were on holiday, despite owing two thousand pounds to a moneylender capable of sending enforcers to collect by any means necessary.

They were married. There was no way out.

Charlotte's head swam. Now she would never know what a love match might be like.

That fantasy wasn't the only thing to be ripped away. She'd also been robbed of free will by the overly helpful Scots law. Marriage was to be one of the few facets in her life where she might have been able to decide something for herself. Gone. Now she would be the property of a stranger. *This* stranger.

Blind with panic, she shut her eyes and tried to breathe. *In through the nose, out through the mouth.* Her calming ritual could not change facts, but it always helped her to think. There must be a silver lining.

Mr. Fairfax cleared his throat. "The real problem is…"

She fought to keep hold of her serenity. "None of what you've already said is a problem?"

"The bigger problem," he conceded with a wince, "is that, legally, what's yours is now mine. And what's mine can legally be seized to pay my debts. Such as your jewelry."

She froze, then touched one of her ruby earrings with trembling fingers. "*No.*"

"I'm afraid so." The barrister gave her a kindly expression. "The law of coverture states that a husband and wife are, legally speaking, one person—consolidated under the husband. Mr. Fairfax cannot give your jewels and money back, because you can no longer own anything separate from him. I'm afraid he's right. If Mr. Fairfax is forced to surrender all valuable objects in his possession to pay a debt, your jewelry is now *his* jewelry, and therefore subject to surrender."

"No," she gasped, touching her jewels with trembling fingers. "These are all I have."

Mr. Fairfax nodded, his expression serious. "We can't let that happen."

Not ever. Her throat grew thick with fear. "What do we do?"

"I've bought us a fortnight. At that point, I have to pay up or go to debtors' prison. But that's my kettle of fish. In the meantime, we'll extricate you from the web. Your possessions will be your own."

No, they wouldn't. Mr. Oldfield had just said it was impossible. She tucked her arms about her chest. "How?"

Mr. Fairfax took a deep breath. "However you like. Do you want a divorce? I'll give you any grounds you choose. Accuse me of infertility, infidelity, impotence, disruptive snoring… whatever you please. I will not contest it. We can start the process today. You'll be rid of this nightmare forever."

Would she? Charlotte stared back at him in silence. Her head ached. She hadn't even broken her fast, and was already not only married, but considering divorce.

She turned to Mr. Oldfield. "Can you help us?"

"With a full parliamentary divorce?" The barrister's expression was skeptical. "Do you have the time and money required to achieve one?"

"I don't have any money." She gestured toward Mr. Fairfax. "It all belongs to him now."

He took her hands. "I promise you. If I cannot raise enough blunt to keep me from debtors' prison, I will spend every penny we do have on getting us a clean divorce, so that you aren't bound to me in any shape or form. Claim any grounds you choose."

"Note that the proceedings are both expensive and public," Mr. Oldfield put in. "Only a few cases are tried because it can take two years to pass a private bill of divorcement before parliament and receive full ecclesiastical dissolution. Even if Mr. Fairfax accepts all blame in a criminal conversion adultery case, you will both become social pariahs from that day forward."

Charlotte slid her hands from Anthony's and buried her face in her palms.

Had she not thought, just a few moments ago, that marriage to a gambler who did not fulfill his debts of honor would sink her status to new depths? Divorce would be even worse.

She wouldn't just lose what little social standing she might have. She would be unmarriageable. Even more so than she was now. Once the divorce was final, no respectable man would want her. Most churches wouldn't even perform a wedding ceremony if the bride was a divorcée.

No friends. No husband. No future.

"No." She gazed back at Anthony bleakly. "Divorce leaves me in an even worse position than marriage to you."

He flinched as her blade struck true. "I feared that was the case. Nonetheless, I had to offer. You should have *some* choice in the matter. As much as either of us do."

"It's not entirely your fault," she admitted. His debts were his doing, but the lies to save her reputation… "I went along with the playacting."

"It doesn't matter. We might share the blame for our inadvertent marriage, but my dire straits are not your burden to bear. There has to be…" His face lit. "How about an annulment? Much easier than a divorce, and none of the stigma. If you're worried about the possibility of a future church marriage, I know of no cases where an annulment prevented a bride from—"

"My reputation would still be permanently ruined," she pointed out dully. "We shared a bedchamber after claiming we were married. Last night, it was an innocent lark that I fully intended to deny in the future, should the question ever arise. But an annulment would make an official public record."

"Then you're stuck with me?" he asked quietly.

"We're stuck with each other, I suppose. For the next fortnight." Slowly, deliberately, she calmed her racing pulse. There was time to think. They were in this together for a fortnight, at least. She turned to the barrister. "We do have grounds for annulment, correct?"

Mr. Oldfield lifted his palm. "Again, I cannot advise you to swear to untruths before parliament. But I will mention that full ecclesiastical annulment can be granted on the basis of adultery, consanguinity, insanity at the time of marriage, or non-consummation due to impotence."

"Insanity seems about right," she muttered. "Should we acquire separate accommodation? Would that help us prove non-consummation if necessary?"

He shook his head. "Annulments have been granted to couples who have been married for months.

In your case, it's only a overnight. The point of contention isn't whether you and your husband sleep in the same bed. It's whether he was capable of performing the consummation act."

She turned to Mr. Fairfax. "In that case, our funds would be far better spent buying your debts back and keeping you out of gaol."

"Exactly. With luck, we won't need to worry about pursuing parliamentary intervention."

"Until then, we'll share a bedchamber—but that's *all* we're sharing."

He frowned. "I've no intention of exercising marital rights. Until I'm no longer bound for gaol, my only desire is to buy back my debts."

"I don't just mean… consummation." Charlotte's cheeks flushed. "I mean no physical relations at all. Not even a kiss. Until we know whether we'll still be wed a fortnight from now, we should endeavor to remain strangers."

"Not friends? Even temporarily?" Mr. Fairfax raised a wry brow. "I cannot blame you. Even once you're granted an annulment, I will have done nothing to enrich your life."

"Friends, then," she said, although she suspected opening her heart even a sliver could only lead to heartbreak. "For the next fortnight."

After all, if they did manage to extract him from his gambling debts… What if they could make their marriage work?

The barrister rose from his seat. "You have plenty to discuss, so I shall leave you to determine your fates. Feel free to contact me if I may be of further service. I shall hold this conversation in the utmost privacy."

"Thank you," Charlotte said fervently. "Your concern for privacy in this matter is very much appreciated."

As soon as Mr. Oldfield was out of earshot, Mr. Fairfax let out his breath. "Impotence. If I cannot see my way out of my debts, I will grant you an annulment based on non-consummation due to impotence. I'll claim a horse's hoof caught me in the wrong spot, and I am no longer capable of performing my husbandly duty."

"You'll be a laughingstock," she said, her words soft.

"I'll be in gaol," he corrected grimly.

"And when you got out?" she asked.

He shrugged. "I'll have undergone a miraculous recovery. Too late for our marriage, but not too late to resume one's rakehell ways."

"Of course it'll be too late." She stared at him. Hadn't he listened to the barrister? "You'd be a social pariah."

"Not for being an impotent rakehell. For having spent years rotting in *gaol*." He rubbed the back of his neck and sighed. "That assumes I'm ever released from debtors' prison, of course. A highly improbable circumstance. Which is why my first priority has to be staying out of gaol in the first place."

"And your second priority?" she asked.

His eyes met hers. "Ensuring we can claim non-consummation in the event I fail to repay my debts and must grant an annulment. Or a divorce."

Charlotte nodded slowly. Blasted predicament. He

was right.

Outside of his financial quandary, Mr. Fairfax seemed like a pleasant enough person—certainly the most considerate man of Charlotte's acquaintance—but if it came down to losing both her husband and her possessions or allowing a divorce to shred what little was left of her reputation but getting her life back… Well. She would have to be practical. If he went to gaol for life, she would have to divorce him if they were denied an annulment.

The wisest move would be to guard her heart and her virtue until they had reason to believe he would still be here one month hence. Charlotte would do her best to help him, but she could not afford to become overly attached to a man who was fated to leave her.

He lowered his gaze to her ears and grimaced. "Try not to flash your jewels. Although the debt collectors promised me two weeks, I cannot swear they will be men of their word. But don't worry. I'll straighten things out when we get to London."

Would he? Could anyone? Fear chilled her flesh.

She removed her earrings and curled her trembling fist about them for safekeeping. These were her only ties to her father. To someone who might love her and never leave her. She would protect them with her life.

As much as she missed her mother, Charlotte would not be returning to London until she found her father.

No matter what it took.

Chapter 5

As Charlotte stepped out of her rented guest chamber and into the corridor, the posting house no longer resembled the sanctuary she'd believed it to be the day before. When she'd thought herself on the cusp of a wonderful new life.

Her world was now perfectly upended. The dreams she'd held on to for so long, the plans she'd painstakingly made for her future… Her temples throbbed. She couldn't think about her future until she had determined what she was going to do now.

Finding a northbound coach was no longer urgent, since this was clearly not a moment in which she could make a good impression on her father. Hiring a maid or a hall boy to mind the door as she slept also no longer made sense. For one, it sounded as though she was going to need every penny in her purse.

For two… now she had Mr. Fairfax.

She cast a sidelong gaze at him as they descended

to the ground floor of the inn. A penniless, prison-bound husband. How had her life come to this?

Her stomach was in no mood for oily kippers, but a bit of cheese and a piece of fruit would not be a bad idea. In the worst of cases, she could save them for later.

When she and Mr. Fairfax entered the dining area, Mr. Garman the innkeeper was behind the bar, folding napkins.

He beamed warmly at Charlotte as they approached. "How did you sleep, ma'am?"

"Better than I will tonight," she said with a pained smile. She might never sleep again.

"Oh?" Mr. Garman's eyebrows lifted. "Are you off so soon, then? I can summon you a hack, if the lady requires."

Charlotte glanced at Mr. Fairfax. What *were* their plans for the night? She couldn't bring a husband who was on the run from creditors to meet her father. Nor would she be returning to England. Not when she was this close to a better life. The previous week had been magical in its utter mundaneness. She had *blended in.*

Now that she'd seen what life could be like, she couldn't bear to leave Scotland, where the tentacles of her London reputation could barely reach.

"We'll stay another night." She touched the lumpy jewelry pouches tucked against her ribs. They were the key to finding her father, which she intended to do at the right moment. Once she knew what to do about Mr. Fairfax. She smiled at the innkeeper. "May I bring the money to you in a little while?"

"Oh, yes, ma'am. No problem at all. You and your

husband can stay as long as you like." He motioned toward the sideboard. "Do you fancy some eggs? They're warm from the kitchen."

She shook her head. "I think I need some fresh air to clear my head. If you have an apple, or a bit of cheese…"

"Absolutely. I'll have Mrs. Garman prepare that for you. Just one moment." He disappeared into the kitchen.

As Charlotte stood next to Mr. Fairfax while they waited for the innkeeper's return, she was suddenly uncomfortably aware of her new husband's presence.

By looking at him, one would never guess he was anything but a carefree society gentleman. And likely an accomplished rake. He was so attractive. So self-assured.

A man like that wouldn't have to look far to find his next mistress. Thick chestnut hair tumbled above piercing green eyes. His lithe body was trim, his muscles well defined. Everything about him—from his perfectly tailored waistcoat to his confident swagger—was eye-catching and seductive.

And now he was married to her. She shivered.

What if they *could* make it work? If they somehow extricated him from his gambling debts, marriage to a gentleman like Mr. Fairfax would be a leap so far up from her previous station that the mere idea would have seemed laughable just days before.

Now it was all too serious.

Although they hadn't known it at the time, the previous evening had been their wedding night. What if it had been real? Charlotte licked her lips. She had no doubt that exercising her marital duty with this man would be nothing less than phenomenal.

She shoved the tempting thought away. Lust belonged to her base nature, not to her brain. She was better than that. If they consummated their marriage, annulment would no longer be possible. She could not let that happen. Neither of them was in a position where removing options was a wise choice.

No matter how hard he was to resist.

"Ma'am?" The innkeeper emerged from the kitchen with a parcel wrapped in a scrap of linen. "Here you are. Anything else you need, just ask."

Charlotte almost laughed. Or cried. Sometimes she didn't know what she felt like doing most. If only there was anything that could be done.

"Shall I escort you on your walk?" her new husband asked quietly. "Or would you prefer to take the air alone?"

She handed him the parcel and took his elbow. "Accompany me, please. We may as well get to know each other."

They stepped out of the inn and into the sunlight. Rolling green hills dipped and soared beneath a clear blue sky. A cool breeze rustled the leaves in the trees and ruffled the edge of her bonnet. Mr. Fairfax kept her hand nestled casually in the crook of his arm as if simple morning strolls like these were typical of their everyday routine.

It was the first time Charlotte had walked arm in arm with a gentleman in her life.

As they meandered along the inn's wooden fence, she was surprised to realize how comfortable she felt in his presence.

After years of desperately trying to protect herself from lecherous men, Mr. Fairfax was different than the obscene roués who often propositioned her. He was so open. So honest. He inquired about her thoughts. Seemed to care about her answers. Gave her as much choice as he could in how to live her life.

He treated her as if she were a person in her own right. As if her opinions mattered just as much, if not more, than his. Such chivalrous treatment was heady. Baffling. And irresistible.

She'd never been invited to a dinner party, to a dance, to a carriage ride in Hyde Park. Not because she was poor or unkempt or uneducated, but because she was the daughter of a prostitute. She'd withstood the disparaging vitriol all her life.

Charlotte bit into her apple with a sigh. She could never let him know exactly what kind of woman he'd wed. His loved ones would be appalled. As would he. One did not publicly associate with guttersnipe.

Not men like him.

If Mr. Fairfax knew the truth about her birth, the truth about her utter lack of respectability, the cheery personality she found so magnetic would disappear in a trice. She'd seen it before. He would pull back in disgust, his nose wrinkling as if her mere presence carried the stench of the gutter. It would be he who sought divorce. Her body tensed.

Above all, she could not return to London. Not with him. The closer they drew to the city, the more likely she would be recognized and her lies of omission laid bare.

A pang of regret filled her. He was handsome and amiable and the more time she spent with him, the more she yearned to know him. Out of the bedchamber… and in it. She couldn't have the latter—not if she was going to file for annulment—but she could not repudiate their attraction. Or deny how delightful she found his company.

She might only have a fortnight with this man. To experience a different life. She wanted to live each day of it as his equal. To know, if only for a short time, what it might have been like if she had been born someone else. Someone better. The sort of lady who could attract town gentlemen like him. A woman who deserved marriage proposals and strolls arm in arm with a smitten suitor. This was her one chance to live as if she were the sort of woman a man could be proud to call his wife.

If only for two weeks.

The reality of their ticking clock soured her stomach. She could not eat the rest of her apple. As she tossed the core beyond the shrubbery, three stone of little boy crashed into her from behind.

Mr. Fairfax swooped the ruddy-cheeked lad up and into the air as a half dozen other little boys ran up, laughing.

He set the boy down and ruffled his hair. "Apologize to the lady."

"I didn't mean to bump her." The lad's chapped lip began to tremble. "They was chasing me and I didn't want to give my cheese up, so I was running and looking over my shoulder…"

Quickly, Charlotte knelt to his level. "You like

cheese?"

He nodded, eyes huge.

She glanced at the other boys. "Do you all like cheese?"

Six more wind-chapped faces nodded vigorously.

"That is a happy coincidence, because *I* like cheese, too. In fact, I have some with me right now." She held out her hand to Mr. Fairfax, who immediately placed the innkeeper's parcel in her palm.

The boys stared back at her, wide-eyed.

"Now, the first thing to make clear is that chasing someone who doesn't wish to be chased is unacceptable behavior." She gave them each a stern glance. "Understood?"

They nodded in fascination.

"The second thing we have to make clear is about sharing." She lifted the parcel to her nose and pantomimed inhaling a wondrous aroma. "Sharing is wonderful. You should do so as often as possible. Sharing is also optional. This means that you cannot force anyone else to share. Is that clear?"

More nods. And several longing glances at her parcel.

"Very well, then." She unwrapped the cloth. A generous chunk of cheese rested inside.

The boys gasped and fell to their knees in a half circle about her. The smallest one reached forward, but the one who had been chased knocked the lad's hand aside.

"*No*," he scolded. "You cannot force a lady to share. Remember?"

The younger boy's eyes filled with tears, but he

nodded.

"Very good," Charlotte agreed. "As it happens, I am indeed in the mood to share. Mr. Fairfax, would you help me divide this cheese into… nine pieces?"

Her husband dropped down onto the lawn without the slightest hesitation, as if fashionable gentlemen in cream-colored breeches spent every morning frolicking in dewy grass. He shook out the scrap of linen as if it were a picnic blanket, and divided the hunk of cheese into even sections.

Charlotte lifted her palms. "I wish we had more cheese to share, but this is all we brought. I daresay we have enough for everyone to have a taste."

The boy who had been chased hesitated, then pushed a tiny chunk of cheese no bigger than one of the nine portions toward Charlotte. "I want to share mine, too. But just with you."

"I accept your kind gift," she said solemnly. "Thank you. And the rest of you? Do you accept my gift?"

Seven grubby hands shot forward to snatch their bit of cheese from the cloth. With a wink in her direction, Mr. Fairfax did the same.

She turned to the boy who had been chased. "Do you have a mama at home?"

He nodded. "She makes the cheese."

Charlotte lifted her untouched portion from the cloth and placed it into the boy's hand. "You can eat this yourself, or you can share it with her. It is your choice."

He scrambled to his feet and started to run.

"Beat you to the river," he called over his shoulder

to the other lads.

The boys launched themselves up to give chase. In no time, they disappeared down the hill.

Mr. Fairfax slanted her an impressed look. "You handled that lot astonishingly well."

"Did I?" Charlotte couldn't help but laugh. "I'm not certain if I managed them or if they managed me. Which one of us gave up our cheese?"

"I am convinced you always had the upper hand. You would have made a splendid governess." He chuckled, then sent her a curious glance. "Have you… ever been a governess?"

A laugh bubbled in her throat at the absurdity of the idea. She'd never had the opportunity. Or even a letter of recommendation. As far as society was concerned, she had nothing to recommend her.

"No," she answered instead. "I have never had employment of any kind."

"Nor I." He leaned against the fence and gave a mock shudder. "It sounds appalling."

She tried to keep her lips from curving. "I am not surprised to hear you say so. I suppose you consider yourself a pink of the ton?"

"Only when I can afford a tailor." A shadow crossed his handsome face. "Have you forgotten how handy I am with needle and thread?"

She blinked. "I thought you were teasing. Or at least exaggerating."

"Did my work with your dresses look as if I was teasing?" His words were light, but the darkness hadn't left his eyes.

Charlotte recalled her surprise at his impeccable

skill with an iron. Even she could not have done a better job.

"No," she admitted. "You're right. I didn't think it through."

He lifted a shoulder. "How about you? Is your family humble or well-to-do?"

Both, she supposed. Any man who could give away rubies must be wealthy beyond imagine. Her mother, however…

Life as the daughter of a courtesan hadn't been easy, but they'd never lacked for any material necessities. One of her mother's many protectors had paid for the townhouse. Another paid for a few servants. Yet another gave them a small line of credit at a modiste who was willing to sew even for a light-skirt of dwindling popularity.

Charlotte had tried not to feel reduced by the judgment of others, but everything from their bonnets to their daily bread had always depended on her mother entertaining another client.

But she'd *had* that daily bread. She'd never once doubted its presence on the morrow. Her life had been miserable due to their position in society, not because they lacked coin.

Somehow she didn't feel right saying such things aloud. Not to a man who'd had to learn to mend hems and iron dresses.

"I came to Scotland to find my father," she admitted instead.

He brightened. "And have you?"

"Not yet. I must be close, however. My father is a laird, so he must be well known." And well respected.

She prayed she would not disappoint.

"That's wonderful." His green eyes lit up. "I adore my family and cannot imagine a world without them in it. You absolutely must meet him. What is his name? How can I help?"

Charlotte shook her head rather than respond. He had to sort his own troubles before she'd be ready to present him to her father. She would want them both to make a good impression.

The fledgling hope building in her breast was more than ill-advised. The last thing she needed was Mr. Fairfax becoming involved. Not when she had no idea what their future held.

But what if they were able to resolve his debts and then discovered they suited quite well? Wouldn't it be lovely to have her father *and* a kind, handsome husband?

She pushed the tantalizing idea away. He couldn't meet her father now. Not with gaol hanging over his head. For now, they must stick to being friends.

"Help me to my feet, Mr. Fairfax," she said instead.

"Oh, dear," he gasped in mock horror. "Are we to be a *stuffy* married couple?"

She looked down her nose at him primly. "A lady would never use her husband's given name without permission."

"Then, by God, you must call me Anthony immediately. And I shall call you…"

She gazed back at him placidly.

"…Mary?" he guessed.

She pressed her lips together and shook her head.

"Sarah? Jane? Griselda Louise?"

She burst out laughing. "Do I look like a Griselda Louise?"

"I have an aunt named Griselda Louise and she's even prettier than you are," he said with an exaggerated harrumph. He held out a palm. "You are quite a judgmental bit of baggage, for someone named… Gertrude Hortense?"

"Charlotte," she admitted as she placed her hands in his. "You may call me Charlotte."

Perhaps his arms were too strong or her knees too weak, but when he pulled her to her feet, she found herself fully in his embrace, her parted mouth mere inches from his.

"Charlotte," he said softly, as if trying the syllables out on his tongue. He wrinkled his nose. "A rather hideous name, but I suppose one cannot help what one is born to."

She smacked his shoulder, but did not remove herself from his embrace. She wasn't certain she even could. Her breasts were molded to his waistcoat, her fingers clinging to hard muscle. If she lifted her chin any higher, her lips would brush against his.

Desire surged within her. The more she tried to deny it, the stronger it became. He was so close. She didn't want him to kiss her because she knew she'd like it. Likely press against him and beg for more, with every beat of her low-born heart. Lust was in her blood. Even though he was within her reach, she knew she should not give in to those desires.

Yet she couldn't make herself pull away.

"We should go back inside," she whispered.

"It's… dangerous out here."

"Very." He cupped a hand behind her head and crushed his mouth to hers.

Sensation flooded her. His lips were soft, warm, firm. With his mouth on hers, he seemed bigger than before. Less safe. More tempting. His warm body was tight with coiled strength. As if he were holding himself back, preventing his carnal side from pouncing. Her blood pulsed with excitement. What must it be like to be on the receiving end of his unchecked passion?

She was breathless in his arms. His kiss was sweetness and power. He well knew he could claim her. He was choosing to woo her.

Shame shimmered beneath her desire. The fact that he could claim her if he wished to was due to the carnal nature she'd spent her life trying to deny. She did not want him to suspect how much he tempted her. And yet she could think of nothing more than losing herself in this kiss.

If the Scottish wind was cool, she couldn't feel it. Every inch of her skin danced with the electricity of his touch. Her flesh was hot, yearning for something she couldn't quite name. Something she was certain only he could give.

He released her forcibly from his embrace, as if to hold her for a single moment more would be to surrender himself completely.

She struggled to regain her equilibrium. Her pulse still sang, her body longing for his touch. His self-control had saved them both. She was just as wanton as she'd always feared. The moment his lips had touched hers, she'd forgotten about stopping. About doing the right thing.

All she wanted was more.

Chapter 6

C*harlotte.* Anthony placed her hand in the crook of his arm and casually strolled along the lawn as if his every fiber wasn't screaming out for him to scoop her into his arms and carry her straight back to the bedchamber.

Soon. He rolled his shoulders.

Once he was a free man, he would give Charlotte a proper marriage. In and out of the bedchamber. They might not have chosen each other, but now that they were stuck together—the idea of losing her held little allure. She was his Lady Luck. The sort of woman a man didn't let go.

Yet he had no business even fantasizing about what a true relationship might be like. He would not deserve a wife until he had paid every penny of his debt.

Anthony angled his chin. He was confident that he would avoid prison—he always managed to pull out of his scrapes unscathed—but, for her sake, he would have to leave every avenue open, from annulment to divorce. Just in case.

Although terminating their union would destroy her reputation in the process, she would not be stripped of her belongings and bound forever to a prisoner. He would not add leaving a penniless wife behind to his list of sins. Destroying his own life was one thing. If he were not there to protect her, it was even more vital that her money and her possessions remain in her control.

That was no future at all.

His fingers clenched. How he wished this were a different kind of outing! If he were going to have a wife, why couldn't they have met during better times? He could imagine how different the courtship might've been if he'd been flush enough to have one. Stealing a kiss atop the natty phaeton he'd had to sell to finance his trip north. At the best clothier in London, where he'd give her modiste carte blanche to create as many gowns for the Season as the lady wished.

Money. It always came back to money. Something he rarely possessed.

He was not at all surprised that the way he'd got a wife was because she hadn't even realized she was entering into a contract. It wasn't at all how he'd hoped it would happen. He'd imagined wooing his future bride with operas, parlors overflowing with flowers, the promise of a palace fit for a queen.

In every dream, his future wife was not only thrilled… she chose him. A woman so lovely inside and out that she could have her pick of the ton—and she would choose Anthony. She needed him. He made her happiest. He was worthy of her love.

Instead, all he'd done for Charlotte so far was ruin her plans and come perilously close to ruining her life. What would he do if the debt collector's ruffians took her jewelry and savings by force? What would he do if he never found any money, and they made good on their promise to send him to Marshalsea prison? What would happen to Charlotte then?

His stomach twisted. He only wanted the best for her, but had accidentally given her his worst.

"Where are you from?" he asked.

She hesitated, then answered, "London."

London. Same as him.

A terrible thought struck him. What if she'd had a beau back home—wherever home was? He hadn't even thought to ask. He rubbed the back of his neck in frustration. What if she had been betrothed? Or promised to the Church? Or had been perfectly happy as an independently wealthy woman of leisure until he came along and stole her independence away? He came to a sudden stop.

"Was there someone else?" he asked her roughly. "Is your heart… are you promised elsewhere?"

"No," she said. Her chin dipped down. "I have no one."

Relief coursed through him. "You *had* no one," he said gruffly. "Now you have me."

She shook her head. "I meant my heart isn't spoken for. My mother lives in London. I hated to leave her, but it was the only way to find my father."

"My mother lives in London, too." He smiled back

at her, irrationally pleased her heart was still free. "My parents' townhouse is in Mayfair. They can't bear to be too far from fashionable things."

Charlotte made no reply.

"We should *try* to get to know one another," he suggested, after the awkward silence stretched on for minutes. "Your heart may not be promised, but surely you've thought about your future. Have you always dreamed of bearing many children?"

"What?" she choked. "No. Why would you ask that?"

"You were good with those hellions," he pointed out.

She shook her head. "You were also quite good with the children."

"I have two nephews," he admitted. "Still a bit younger than those lads, but already tremendous terrors. Identical twins. I'm one of the few who can tell them apart."

She smiled. "They sound lovely. Do you see them often?"

Not often enough. He sighed.

"I visit every time I have a lucrative evening at the tables. I love to bring them little boats, paints, wooden horses… Their eyes light up when my carriage pulls in the drive, because they know there's a treat for them inside."

Or they had. Back when he'd had a carriage. And lucrative evenings at the tables.

Her eyes softened. "I'm sure you're their favorite uncle."

"I should expect so," he said with his haughtiest

sniff. "The other uncle got all the looks. I should at least be the most fun."

"I doubt he got *all* the looks." She waved the idea away. "I'm not nearly as repulsed by your emerald eyes and bedimpled smile as one might presume."

"No?" He turned to her with interest. His heart lightened. "Tell me more about how devastatingly handsome I am. Could you send a short note to the society papers?"

She arched a brow. "I doubt you've suffered any lack of ladies gushing over how attractive you are. Just to be different, I shall admire your character instead. I admit I like the sound of you spoiling your nephews."

He twisted his lips. "Even if I can only do so when luck is in my favor?"

"If you spoiled children every day, they truly would grow up to be terrors." She gave a mock shiver. "It sounds to me as if you do everything you can, whenever you can. The best gift is time, not money. How could anyone ask for more?"

His step faltered. No one had ever viewed his wild swings of fortune and famine in such a positive light before. The idea that someone could see all his faults and still find something in him worth praising had his heart pounding.

A win at the gaming tables over a decade ago had been the first time he'd made his family proud. It had also changed his life. Since then, he had spent his entire life trying to buy love, to buy approval, the one way he knew how.

He had brought Charlotte nothing but trouble. Yet she did not hate him. She even seemed to… like him.

To think that the innocent person who'd borne the worst of his recklessness might still view him as a good, or at least as a reasonably attentive uncle… His chest expanded. Such praise was dizzying. Mystifying. Addicting.

He did not yet deserve it.

Self-recrimination washed over him. He had no business taking pride in a life he had little control over. How different their relationship might have been if he had met Charlotte with his affairs actually in order! He needed to get his situation sorted, and fast. Not just for himself. For her.

But what could he do? The sums he needed…

Anthony did have acquaintance with a fair number of dukes and earls, but he could not possibly misuse their friendship in such a fashion. For many reasons. After all, the man currently in possession of Anthony's IOUs had also once been his friend. Today, the man had sent enforcers.

Someone with a title would be even more persuasive when it came time to repay debts.

He would have to earn the money himself. Somewhere. Somehow. Within the next fortnight.

Only then could he truly begin to be a proper husband. To make Charlotte happy. His jaw tightened. He could think of nothing worse than for the one person who had ever refrained from judging him a useless wastrel to decide she had erred and he was worthless after all. He *had* to come up with something.

"What are you thinking about?" she asked.

"Kissing you," he answered automatically. The act might not have been in the forefront of his mind, but he suddenly realized it had never been far from his thoughts. Not since the moment he'd met her.

"How interesting," she said. "I was recoiling from the horrendous grass stains on the rear of your breeches."

"What's that? You say you were ogling my buttocks?" He peered over his shoulder as if to preen. "I cannot blame you. I'm told it's the finest in England."

"Who told you that?" she teased. "Your mirror?"

He patted her hand where it lay against his arm. "Now, I don't want you to feel bad about *your* ghastly deformity, but I thought I should mention the sharp stabbing pains of whatever is protruding from your ribcage cutting through my waistcoat as I bravely rejected your carnal advances."

Pink flooded her cheeks. "Oh, no. It's the money pouches. I—I forgot they were there."

He nodded gravely. "I often forget affixing multiple heavy purses to my ribcage."

"And a necklace," she added after a moment. "That might have been the lumpiest bit."

He affected a foppish pose. "Lumpy, but iconic. Something to tie the pieces together. Underneath your petticoat."

"As one does," she agreed.

He considered asking her why she would hide ornamentation beneath her clothes, but changed his mind. A man with grass stains on his arse was in no position to criticize the fashion quirks of a lady.

Not for the first time, however, he wondered how much money Charlotte *did* have. Her dazzling jewelry indicated her wealth wasn't unsubstantial. And her willingness to wager an entire purse within moments of joining a gaming table indicated a complete lack of concern about her finances.

He didn't ask, because he didn't need to know. Her finances had nothing to do with his debt. Legalities be damned. Besides, the money a pawnbroker would give them for her jewelry was only a fraction of what he owed. It would be surrendering her most cherished possessions for nothing.

Anthony couldn't let that happen. His top priority was keeping Charlotte safe while he got things sorted.

And then he'd buy her thousands of jewels. All the necklaces and tiaras her heart desired.

Even if she wore them all strapped to her ribcage for safekeeping.

"Your earrings are quite pretty," he said. "What made you decide to wear them on the outside of your petticoat?"

She touched her fingertips to her ear. "They belonged to my father. It's the only jewelry I own. These earrings and the matching necklace had been in his family for generations. He gave them to my mother before they lost contact."

He tried not to groan. The rubies were family heirlooms. That eye-catching jewelry wasn't even *hers*. He couldn't possibly let the debt collectors confiscate them. Charlotte would never get them back and he would still go to prison. "Why don't we return them to your mother? Just until my current situation smooths out."

She shook her head. "I can't. These jewels aren't just my legacy. They're the key to reuniting me with my father."

Splendid.

He let out his breath, completely at a loss for a glib rejoinder… or a plan. It was his duty to ensure her safety, and the safety of her legacy. Under no circumstances could he allow her to be forced to relinquish such treasure.

Except, his creditors had not only managed to find him… Gideon's ruffians knew about Charlotte, too.

Chapter 7

Back aching from hours of hard work, Anthony crawled into bed and collapsed onto the now-familiar mattress with a sigh. This was his fourth morning at the Kitty and Cock Inn. His third as a married man. And his second day of farm labor before the crack of dawn.

In other words, he had come up with a plan.

Short of a series of extraordinary windfalls at the gaming tables every night, a fortnight was not enough time for any reasonable gentleman to raise two thousand pounds.

Anthony knew it. Maxwell Gideon had to know it as well.

The fact that Gideon had permitted a two-week period of grace indicated that, despite being the powerful lord of a vice parlor, their past friendship prevented him from throwing Anthony to the wolves without a fighting chance.

This was good news. This meant there *was* a chance, however slight it might be. Anthony's luck at the gaming tables the previous night had been miserable at best, but that was immaterial. Gideon would not be impressed by sob stories. The only thing that ever impressed him was money.

So Anthony would bring it to him.

Not two thousand pounds, of course. That was impossible. But he would take every job he could and save every penny he earned in order to prove his sincerity. He wouldn't be able to repay Gideon this week or even this month, but he could do so eventually.

Surely that would do. Gideon's enforcers had not been sent to shake the shillings out of Anthony's pockets, but to scare him into taking his debts seriously.

It was as simple as that. Anthony hoped.

His freedom depended on it.

"What time is it?" Charlotte mumbled.

He rubbed his tired face. "Half nine. Go back to sleep."

She wrinkled her nose. "It's late. I should wake up."

Anthony couldn't argue. He couldn't even stay awake. He'd risen before dawn to collect eggs, milk cows, herd sheep—anything any soul in this town was willing to pay for. After luncheon, he had promised to trim hedges around the church. The property wasn't huge, but the hedgerows soared. He'd be lucky to return home before Charlotte was already back in bed.

Home. He covered his face with his hands. Had he just equated the elegant Kitty and Cock Inn with home?

"I miss London," he murmured. "Milking cows and trimming hedgerows is exhausting."

She opened her eyes. "Then why do it?"

Originally, because it was his only hope to buy more time from Gideon. But that was not the only reason. Not anymore. A smile tugged at his lips as he let his arms fall back to his sides.

He did it because the villagers were so *thankful.*

At first, their honest appreciation was confusing. Flattering. But it had become addictive. For the first time in his life, people looked forward to his visits, not because they expected him to arrive bearing monetary gifts for them, but because he was going to make their lives better.

The busy dairy farm with far more cows than milkmaids. The arthritic old farmer who couldn't keep his sheep on his property. The grandmother whose hands were too gnarled to collect eggs without dropping them.

In coin, each could only pay a pittance. But what they paid in smiles and happiness… The rush of answering pleasure in Anthony's veins was second only to the rush of excitement at winning at the gaming tables.

Yet this thrill was different. This wasn't the vagaries of luck, or Lady Fortune. This exquisite high could be counted upon every single time he trimmed a perfect hedge, combed a basket of wool, or delivered a basket of intact eggs.

He felt… he felt… in control of his life, rather than subject to the whims of Fate.

He felt valued.

"I'm good at milking cows," he answered at last.

Charlotte smoothed the blanket up over his chest and then jerked her hands away. She should not touch him like that. "I have no doubt you'd be good at anything you set your mind to doing."

He didn't answer. He couldn't. The thought of being good at something—as opposed to occasionally being lucky—had simply never crossed his mind before. No one had ever expected it of him. Much less assumed he had natural aptitude.

His father had never had a trade, or even a hobby. Nor had his mother. Or his sister. Yet being active members of society was expensive. Ever since Anthony had entered his first gaming parlor as a young lad, the majority of the family fortune had come from gambling.

As had the majority of their misfortune.

If they'd had a cow, or a few chickens, the efforts of their own hands might have alleviated the periods of hunger. There was no room for cows or chickens in Mayfair townhouses, of course, but what the devil was a family like his doing living in a Mayfair townhouse to begin with?

When fortune blessed Anthony at the gaming tables, he and his family lived like royalty for months, or even years, at a time. But when luck was absent, they could not pay their servants or their rent. Long periods of poverty plagued them between months of riches.

He frowned. Such extremes of plethora and paucity could have been avoided. Rather than bounce from lease to lease, from abundance to beggared, never knowing what the morrow might bring, they might have chosen to live more simply. Somewhere in the middle.

That was, if anyone in his family had an ounce of sense when it came to minding the purse strings.

Anthony's sister Sarah flashed into his mind. One might think the Fairfaxes the last family on earth destined to become farmers, but look at his baby sister now. He had thought her and her husband mad when they had given up their fashionable townhouse to move out to the country and raise their boys on a hill by a river. His parents had certainly been horrified.

It didn't sound like madness now. It sounded as though his sister was by far the brightest member of the Fairfax family.

He needed to be as strong as she was. He needed to think about the future, not just live in the moment. He needed to take even greater action.

"I'll find a position," he said aloud. "Reliable employment."

Charlotte's hand stilled over his chest. "More cows and chickens?"

"A trade," he clarified. "Perhaps an apprenticeship."

She jerked her hand from his chest. "You cannot be serious."

He turned toward her. "Why not?"

"No trade on earth pays two thousand pounds per fortnight," she pointed out. "Besides, gentlemen don't work in trade. Your status… your reputation…"

Her rational logic dashed cold water on his plans. Yet it was the only plan they had.

"My societal standing shan't increase much by

contracting gaol fever in debtors' prison," he reminded her flatly. If she and the rest of society liked him less because he had worked as a farmer or a secretary, then so be it. "Where else am I to get money?"

"You can have my savings," she insisted again. "It's not much, but it's legally yours. If it helps keep you out of prison—"

"It's not your debt." He averted his gaze. She was the innocent party. He would solve his problems by himself. "And it's not enough money. Even if we sold your rubies."

She gasped at the idea. "You can't have my jewels. Not until I find my father. Th-they're my only proof that I'm his daughter."

"I'm not asking for them." He stared up at the bed canopy. He hoped it wouldn't come to that.

Her voice shook. "Then what are we going to do?"

"*We* aren't going to do anything. You must remain in the posting houses when I'm not here, in order to keep watch over our savings. After that break-in, I don't trust leaving them unattended. Nor is it a wise idea to carry pound notes and gold coins to a dairy farm."

"It doesn't have to be a farm." She bit her lip. "Perhaps I could find work as a maid or minding children. It would be better than—"

"No. Our money would still be at risk. You can't chase children or scrub a scullery with two earrings, a necklace, and hundreds of pounds strapped to your chest. You'll stay here, where our money's safe and *you're* safe."

"Doing what? Making conversation in the common rooms while you kill yourself under the hot sun to earn a pittance? Why bother, if it won't be enough?"

"It *will* be enough," he said fiercely. "Not to pay off the entire debt at once, but to prove to Gideon I take the threat seriously. His enforcers refused to consider paying back the debt in installments, but Gideon is my friend. If I go to him next week with twenty or thirty percent in hand, he'll give me more time."

Possibly.

He hoped.

Hope filled Charlotte's eyes. "Truly? You are certain?"

Anthony wasn't certain of anything anymore. He rolled over into his pillow rather than lie to Charlotte.

Besides, what was left to say? He would return every penny, no matter how long it took him to earn them. Even if it meant sweating in a coal mine. Even if it took years.

Even if it meant having to annul their marriage to keep her safe.

When he awoke a few hours later, Charlotte was no longer at his side. He forced himself out of bed and over to the washbasin to splash cold water onto his face.

He didn't have to wonder where Charlotte had gone. Unable to toil in fields or otherwise raise funds to put toward Anthony's debt, she felt powerless to help him.

She was frustrated with him, he knew, for not accepting her meager savings to use toward his debts. But in the event that he was unable to save himself after all, he refused to leave her penniless. He well knew what it was like to go days between meals. He would never willfully consign another person to such misery. His wife least of all. Rather, his ex-wife. If there were no saving himself from gaol, the least he could do was save Charlotte from being shackled to *him*.

As soon as he was clean and dressed, Anthony headed downstairs to find her. He only had a few moments to spare before his appointment to trim the church's hedgerows, but he disliked the idea of departing with so much unresolved between them. Charlotte was clearly afraid the situation was not under control.

He had to prove to her that it was.

As he reached the foot of the stairs, a wave of boos and laughter near the front door caught his attention. Curious, he stepped forward to see what the ruckus was about.

A handful of gentlemen crowded against the open window, pointing at a bashful female sheep who was deftly sidestepping the amorous advances of her would-be white-wooled lover.

"Ten quid says the ewe will outfox him," shouted one of the men.

"Twenty quid says she'll give in," cried another. "That ram is a handsome one."

"Fairfax!" exclaimed a third. "Come and look. Is your money on the tup or the cut direct?"

"Cut direct," he replied without hesitation. "Females are mysterious creatures, and stronger than you think."

"Fairfax put twenty on utter rejection?" crowed the first man. "I told you I was right!"

"I raise you to thirty," said the second. "That ram is a force who will not be denied. Just look at the way he—"

"Ohhh," the men exclaimed as the ewe abruptly submitted to temptation. "That beast cuts a swath through his flock, he does!"

An upside-down top hat tapped against Anthony's chest. "Everyone who wagered on the ewe's strength of character, put your money in the hat."

Laughing at the ridiculous scene, Anthony reached into his pocket for his gambling purse… and caught sight of Charlotte staring at him in disbelief from just outside the dining room. The disappointment on her pale face hit him like a blow to the chest.

His hand froze on his purse. Shame washed over him.

He had made hundreds of such idle wagers. Thousands, perhaps. A spot of nonsense between gentlemen, meant as nothing more than a moment of thoughtless fun.

But he didn't have the right to be thoughtless anymore. Or reckless or impulsive or any of his other previously defining characteristics. Not when he was ten days away from being tossed into Marshalsea. He needed to be hoarding every penny, not throwing twenty quid away on the whims of a sheep in heat.

Such wagers were how he had fallen into this mess. His only hope for climbing out of it was proving this was no longer who he had been. That he could be responsible with money. That Gideon could trust Anthony to repay his debt. That Charlotte could count on him not to leave her alone and destitute.

He broke eye contact with her long enough to count his sovereigns into the hat. His neck heated with shame. This was the last time, he ordered himself fiercely. He was better than that. Or should be. When had gambling become as natural to him as breathing, such that he no longer even noticed the risks he was taking?

Not anymore. Now he had Charlotte. And the very real risk of prison. A man in his position could not afford to gamble away so much as tuppence.

Not when his entire life was on the line.

Chapter 8

Later that evening, Charlotte sat in the inn's dining room awaiting Anthony's return.

Before leaving to trim hedges, he had begged her forgiveness for the asinine wager she'd happened to see him make. She had waved away his apology as if the incident meant nothing.

It meant everything.

Bearing witness to how wholly irresponsible he was with his finances served to underscore how carefully she needed to guard her heart. Even if they managed to save him from prison, how could she be certain it wouldn't happen again? She hugged herself and pushed the worry aside.

First things first.

She would do everything in her power to help him, but if they could not raise the money—or if he lost it all on a spurious wager—she would find herself alone and husbandless. It didn't matter how kind or charming he was. He would rot in Marshalsea and she would be powerless to stop it.

Her entire savings were less than ten percent of what he owed, yet it was all they had. She touched the money pouch hidden beneath her shift. Although she was the disrespectable one, her financial situation was far more stable than his. Her shoulders slumped.

What if they did save Anthony from gaol only for him to amass staggering debt all over again? Had he learned a valuable lesson, or would he keep on gambling?

"I just don't know," the anxious governess seated across from her continued. "What do you think I should do?"

Charlotte forced her mind back to the present. This young woman had come to Charlotte for help after overhearing Charlotte's comments to some of other ladies in the drawing room. She straightened her shoulders. Solving other people's problems was far easier than addressing her own.

"It sounds to me as if you should definitely take the Banfield opportunity once Timothy comes of age. If Agnes decides to stay in Edinburgh as a governess, that is her business. I see no reason why you should be forced to mind a nursery if you dislike doing so. Not if your talents are more suited to being a paid companion, and you already have a position waiting."

The young lady sagged with relief. "Then that's precisely what I'll do. You are so wise, Mrs. Fairfax. Thank you ever so much for your counsel."

At the words *Mrs. Fairfax*, a shiver danced along

Charlotte's skin. She still couldn't quite believe she was married. Only in Scotland could her life have taken such an extraordinary turn.

After the governess excused herself from the table, an increasingly familiar presence settled on the bench beside Charlotte. Even with purple smudges beneath his eyes, Anthony Fairfax remained breathtakingly handsome. Her heart leaped, despite her best attempt to remain impartial.

He kissed the back of her hand, then lifted his chin toward the retreating governess. "Who was that?"

"Future paid companion." Charlotte raised her eyebrows. "How were the hedgerows?"

"Tall." His smile reached his eyes. "You could make a business of that, you know."

"Hedgerows?"

"Helping people."

She furrowed her brow. "How is helping people a business? If we take tea at the same table and they happen to tell me their troubles… You can't expect them to pay a total stranger for her opinions on the matter."

"A stranger over tea, no," he agreed. "But if you had an office like a secretary or a barrister, and you were renowned as an expert in providing unbiased perspective and common-sense steps to take action on domestic matters, I am convinced you could be a rich woman."

She tilted her head in interest. This was a very good sign. Perhaps he was finally ready to accept her help. "I thought you didn't want my money."

"I don't." He leaned back in his chair. "That doesn't mean you should ignore your own finances.

And besides, you are incredible. You should be rewarded for it."

"By whom?" she scoffed. "No one would pay for common sense."

He lifted an eyebrow. "This is apparently going to come as quite a shock to you, my dear, but… not everyone possesses common sense. In fact, the more fashionable the lady, the less becoming it is to have anything at all between her ears." His tone was light, but his eyes were surprisingly serious. "I am fortunate indeed to have found a woman with both beauty and brains."

As warm as his faith in her made her feel, she couldn't imagine society taking a lady barrister seriously, much less a woman like her, dispensing nothing more than common sense.

"We need a plan," she said instead. "A real one. If I had two thousand pounds, I would force you to take it. We only have a week and a half left."

"I have a plan. I told you this morning." His eyes looked tired. "I'm going to be an apprentice."

Frustration gnawed at her. "An apprentice egg gatherer? An apprentice dairymaid?"

"Not here, of course. London." He ran a hand through his hair. "My friends and family are there, as are a lot of well-connected people. Most of *le bon ton*, in fact. Which is perfect. High society is our only hope."

A chill shivered down her spine. No. She could never return to London. Not only was it her personal hell, but she had no wish for Anthony to witness what the real world truly thought about her.

Besides, she didn't see how a ten-day apprenticeship would solve anything. Or how his acquaintances would help him procure one. The more well-connected his friends, the less likely they were to dirty their gloves.

She shook her head. "It won't work. Society doesn't dabble in trade."

"Not directly," he agreed. "But who designs our clothing? Who distributes the coal? Who builds the looms?"

No respectable gentleman, that was certain. And not Anthony. Not before time ran out. "You want to be… a modiste? A factory worker? A miner?"

He sighed. "Perhaps none of those avenues is the perfect choice."

"Thank heavens," she muttered. The farther they were from the city, the better. He would have ruined his standing and still not earned enough money.

"The point is," he continued, "well-connected people tend to know other well-connected people. Dukes and marquesses may not have a trade themselves, but they do invest their money in projects they deem lucrative. One of *those* is liable to have an opening of some sort. An apprenticeship, a secretary. I would earn more in a day than I could here all year. Apart from the gaming tables, it's our best chance at real money. We should leave at first light. We'll… We'll come back for your father."

No. She couldn't lose her chance at finding her father! Panic gripped her. She had no wish to return to the snubs and degradation. She could not bear to have Anthony look at her with the same disgust.

Once she found her father, things would be different. She assumed the laird would have to present her as a long-lost poor relation rather than his bastard daughter, but that was no problem. It was *respectable.* She would no longer have to feel ashamed.

"My father is here," she said, her heart beating frantically. "I came this far. I don't want to leave before finding him."

He frowned in visible irritation. "You do not approve of going to London, yet you will not let me assist you with finding your father. What am I supposed to do, Charlotte?"

"*You* go to London," she blurted. "I'll find him on my own, and then find you."

"I'm not abandoning my wife alone in a foreign country."

"It's… Scotland," she reminded him. And the only place she felt safe. Or anonymous.

"Scotland is no safer than England. You'll still be a woman alone, and I'll still be responsible for your safety." He leaned forward, brow furrowed. "Why won't you let me help you find your father?"

She gazed back at him for a long moment. At his kindness, his eagerness to help, the much-deserved pride he took in surviving another long day of menial labor. Perhaps he was right. Some assistance would be useful. After all, the longer they stayed in Scotland, the less she had to worry about going back to London. Besides, Anthony might be a huge help. He knew so many people. The uncertainty could be over within days.

At first, she hadn't wanted her father to meet her new husband, for fear Anthony wouldn't live up to her father's standards. But whose standards truly mattered? If she could tell a governess to never mind her sister's life and concern herself with living her own, then surely Charlotte could take a spoonful of her own medicine.

Perhaps this was even the way out. Her father was wealthy enough to give expensive jewels to a prostitute without a second thought. What might he do for his own flesh and blood? Not a gift. A loan. Charlotte would ensure they paid back every penny.

And if her father insisted upon providing the money as a dowry instead… Hope blossomed. She reached for her husband's hand. Such a miracle could save Anthony's life—and their marriage. Which became more and more real with each new day.

They might not have chosen each other, but, as each hour in his company passed, she dreaded the moment ever more when his creditors might take him from her.

Besides, if she were honest, her true concern wasn't about her father rejecting Anthony. A laird would be willing to overlook a gentleman's lack of fortune. It was whether her father would accept *her*. Anthony was high society. Charlotte was not, and nobody knew it better than her father. But, oh, how she longed to be.

However, by avoiding confrontation, she realized with a frown, she wasn't protecting herself or Anthony. The truth was, she was procrastinating because, somewhere inside, she was still the same scared little girl she'd always been. Afraid of being laughed at. Of being turned away. Afraid of never being good enough to overcome her past. Afraid even her father wouldn't love her.

But she shouldn't be. The laird was just as responsible for her regrettable status as her mother, was he not? He could scarcely blame a child for an act he chose to perform two-and-twenty years ago. She was a woman now. An adult. And she hadn't come this far just to cower in the corner. Too much depended on her courage.

"All right." She gave Anthony a shaky smile. "You can help me. I appreciate your assistance. Thank you for asking."

He leaned forward and kissed the top of her head. "What are indulgent husbands for?"

"Herding sheep?" she guessed nervously.

"Only in the mornings." He squeezed her hand. "Please. I want to help you find your father. At least tell me his name."

Her pulse steadied. Yes. This was a good plan. If anyone could help her, it was Anthony.

She took a deep breath, then nodded sharply. "Dìonadair."

Anthony blinked in confusion. "He's a protector?"

She sighed in exasperation. "No, he's a laird. My father has noble blood. He…"

He's a protector? Her explanation trailed off as a deep sense of foreboding sank into her stomach. Her husband was not the first to use a word generally reserved for men who paid courtesans for sensual favors. Yet she had never once mentioned her past to Anthony. How could he know about her mother's history? How long had he known who she really was?

"Why?" she demanded. "Why would you say that?"

"I..." He blinked at her. "Well, you said *dìonadair*. I don't claim to be an expert in Gaelic, but I always thought that word meant 'protector.' Or perhaps 'defender.' Why, is it relevant? Is *dìonadair* a clue?"

Her blood ran cold. *Dìonadair* meant protector?

It wasn't a clue, Charlotte realized with sinking dread. It was a lie. A bald, calculated lie told to a frightened little girl who wanted desperately not to believe she was worthless. A lie to hide her father's identity.

The man was no more than one of her mother's many paying clients.

She had no one. There was nobody to find.

"Dìonadair was supposed to be his name," she said hollowly, as she realized her dreams were as unsubstantial as smoke... dissipating quickly, leaving only a stench behind. "My noble father, the laird. My hero never existed."

"I could be wrong," Anthony said hastily. "Perhaps—perhaps Dìonadair is the second most common surname in Scotland. I wouldn't know. I'm not a Scot. We could ask—"

She shook her head. It was so painfully obvious, now that she viewed the facts with the eyes of an adult rather than the eyes of a child. There *were* no facts. She was exactly what people had been telling her all along: nothing.

I see you found your dìonadair, *lassie.*

That's what the drunkard had said when he'd caught them in the corridor. The drunkard who had undoubtedly overheard her in the common area earlier, saying she was looking for an older gentleman, a *dìona-dair*.

Laird, preferably.

She clapped a hand over her mouth to stifle a horrified, choking laugh. In her innocent quest to save her reputation, she'd only managed to make it even worse. And for what? Approbation she should have known she could never have?

Anthony reached for her shoulder. "Charlotte…"

She jerked away. She couldn't stand his touch right now. Couldn't stand her own skin. Her willful naivety. Her determination to believe in a fantasy. Embarrassment heated her cheeks. What did she know about her alleged father other than he was supposed to be a laird called Dìonadair, from Scotland? Wouldn't there have been more information other than his legendary angelic goodness, if any of it had been real?

The rubies. God only knew where the rubies had come from. Undoubtedly one of her mother's admirers. But obviously not from a Scottish laird named Dìonadair. There was no such man. She had no father.

"You can have the jewels," she said dully. She yanked the bobs from her ears and flung them in Anthony's direction. "They're meaningless. It all is."

Her lungs heaved as she fought against the stinging in her eyes. In her dreams, Scotland was meant to be paradise. Her father's homeland. Perhaps her future home, too.

She had come all this way for love, for acceptance. Her father was to be the one person capable of sweeping her past under the rug. Of giving her a fresh start. A respectable name. A home.

Miss Charlotte Dìonadair she'd called herself, all those long, lonely nights, trying to pretend she couldn't hear the noises coming from her mother's chamber.

Charlotte Dìonadair was the daughter of a laird. Beautiful. Practically a princess. Charlotte Dìonadair was allowed into all the shops. Charlotte Dìonadair could play with all the other children. Charlotte Dìonadair was proud to speak her name.

Charlotte Dìonadair was more than respectable… Charlotte Dìonadair was beloved.

Charlotte Dìonadair was a lie.

Dreams. Useless, foolish dreams. When they vanished, her heart shattered with them. There would be no happy ever after for her. She swallowed brokenly.

Welcome back to reality. She wasn't the daughter of a laird, or a beautiful princess. She wasn't allowed into all the pretty places. She couldn't rub shoulders with those above her station. She wasn't proud to speak her name. She didn't even *have* one.

Her mother was a whore and a liar. Which meant she hadn't the least idea who Charlotte's father was.

And now Charlotte never would either.

Chapter 9

Charlotte's pulse pounded in her ears. The dawning realization on her husband's face was all too clear.

"You've never known who your father was." He leaned back. Away from her. "You're…"

"A bastard," she said beneath her breath. "Yes."

He licked his lips. "Charlotte—"

She pushed away from the dining table before her husband could ask any more questions she didn't want to answer. Once again, she was a spectacle. Unable to bear the other guests staring at her, she stumbled through the corridors and into their small chamber.

Anthony joined her in silence, her discarded earrings in his palm.

She couldn't bear to look at him. Not after seeing her like this. What a fool he must think her, to follow a dream only a child's blind faith could believe in. A fiction her mother had sold her.

The necklace she'd been proud of for years now bit into her skin like a swarm of ants. She had to get it off. Never wanted it to touch her again.

She pulled up her skirt in order to reach the binding round her ribs.

Anthony turned away to grant her privacy.

It didn't matter. Her desperation wasn't about him. It was about getting rid of the poisonous lie she'd been carrying next to her heart.

She yanked the necklace out from under the binding cloths and hurled the rubies onto the dressing table. She pulled the money pouches free as well and threw them next to the necklace. Their winnings couldn't help her. She was just what she'd always been—the daughter of a prostitute. With no father and nowhere to go.

Shivering, she unwrapped the linen binding her breasts and tossed it aside. No more hiding. She was who she was. There was no sense trying to playact any longer.

She let her skirt fall to the floor, then turned toward the looking glass. The masking powder she had always added to her hair to make it dull and lifeless, the subtle face paint she had used every morning to make her complexion tired and gray and less like her mother's... What did any of it matter?

It took very little of the icy water in the basin to wash away what she'd spent a lifetime trying to hide.

She was not her father's daughter. She was her mother's. They were two sides of the same coin. The same rosy cheeks and golden ringlets that had made her wide-eyed mother so irresistible to men stared right back at Charlotte in the mirror.

Her shoulders crumpled. She could run away from home, flee those who spat at her in the street—if they acknowledged her at all—but she could never escape her own reflection.

She jerked away from the looking glass and directed her wooden legs toward a wingback chair. Its cushions no longer comforted her. She was no longer on a path to adventure and approval. She was adrift at sea.

Anthony knelt by the fireplace to coax steady flames from the embers. But the warmth did not reach her.

She stared listlessly at the grate. What would become of her now? The sole hope on her horizon had been stripped away. While her father's money was meant to save Anthony, her father's love was meant to save Charlotte.

Her gaze inexorably traveled toward her husband. Her heart sank. It would be foolish to develop an attachment to him. He, too, would be taken from her before long.

Then she would have no one. Just like before.

He pulled the chaise longue next to her chair and settled beside her.

She said nothing. She couldn't trust herself to. If she spoke, she might shatter.

"I'm sorry we can't find your father," he said quietly.

She closed her eyes. "I don't have one."

"You did," he said. "Once. Everyone did. If he chose not to stay, I'd say you were better off without someone like that in your life."

"Of course you would say that," she said through clenched teeth. He had undoubtedly been loved and flattered all his life. "You *have* your parents. Both of them. You can't possibly know what it was like for me as a child. No one does."

"Then tell me," he said simply.

Ah. If only it were that simple.

Charlotte stared at the dancing flames until her vision blurred orange. How was she supposed to tell him? She'd never told anyone. She'd hidden beneath makeup and layers of cloth. Lied about her name, her heritage, anytime she was somewhere she might not be recognized. Cleaved to the idea of a man who had never existed.

"Even the poorest children were better than me," she said at last. Her voice was as unsteady as her pulse.

Anthony kept his silence.

"We didn't live in the worst parts of London. We had too much money for that—yet not enough respectability to live anywhere fashionable. So we lived where we could. On streets where the others couldn't be too choosy about who their neighbors were. Yet next to houses where the children didn't just know who their parents were… They lived together. As a family."

The crackling of the fire was the only sound.

"*Charlotte the harlot,*" she singsonged with a harsh laugh. "That was my name growing up. Because that's what my mother was. A light-skirt. A fancy one."

Anthony brushed the back of her hand with his own.

Her breath caught at the gentle touch. How could he have compassion? She was telling him he was married to a prostitute's bastard daughter! Suddenly the words came tumbling out.

"The life of a courtesan is only glamorous while she's out at the opera, riding in fast carriages, presiding at balls, twirling beneath the stars in a gown to rival a princess. But her home is never her home. It's a place of negotiation. The give and take of power. Mother lost her edge because she was saddled with me."

He frowned as if he'd never given much thought to a courtesan's private life before. He probably hadn't. No man ever did.

Or was he frowning because he just realized what a huge mistake he'd made by leg-shackling himself to *her*? Charlotte's throat tightened.

"One of the first things I learned was that there are good clients and there are bad clients. Some would leave me a treat or a dolly. Others…" Her voice cracked. "Sometimes it was best to stay under the bed, or in a dark corner of my wardrobe."

His eyes filled with sympathy.

She dropped her gaze so she wouldn't have to meet his. The memories suffocated her. She'd tried so hard to forget.

"The one thing I wanted was to be respectable. To be accepted. The one thing I didn't want was to be anything like my mother. No matter how much I love her." Her throat rasped. "Sometimes the gowns and jewels she wore were dazzling to the eyes. At other times, her only adornment was bruises on her wrists or her face."

He winced and reached for her.

She pulled away. If he touched her, she would not be able to stop the tears. And if she let herself fall apart, she might not be able to put herself back together.

"I don't know how old I was when I realized I would never be respectable. That no matter how well I succeeded in my quest not to follow my mother's footsteps, it would never be enough. I'm not just a bastard. I'm a whore's by-blow. A mistake. No man would want me as anything other than what I'd been born to be. No ladies would lower themselves to accept my friendship, for the slightest association with me could lower their reputations as well. The only person who would ever love me was my mother."

He made no objections to these claims. No false attempt to insist she was valuable, desirable. Respectable. They both knew she was not. She appreciated his honesty. Even if it made her shrivel inside. She had wanted Anthony to like her. Had let herself believe in the fantasy they'd created of a respectable newlywed couple. Had desperately yearned for the lie to be true.

She risked a glance up at him through her lashes. He hadn't stormed off in disgust, but that didn't mean he wasn't plotting to leave. Why should he stay? They weren't a real couple. Now they would never be.

Before, they had planned for an annulment only if he couldn't avoid debtors' prison. After this conversation, Anthony wouldn't want to wait even a fortnight.

Yet he deserved to know the truth.

"At some point, I latched on to the idea of a father. The baker's daughter, the cobbler's daughter, the fishmonger's daughter—they were all not only more respectable than me, but they also knew who they were. They had someone's arms to come home to. A family. A future." Her voice broke. "I wanted that, too. But I couldn't have it. Not as me."

His eyes were dark with sympathy.

She couldn't look at him. Couldn't acknowledge his empathy. Sympathetic gazes couldn't change her situation. Nothing could. No matter how hard she wanted it.

"I was small when my mother gave me that jewelry. The strongbox was hidden in my wardrobe, not hers. The rubies fascinated me. Once she realized her mistake, how desperate I was to find my father, she commanded me never to seek him, and then refused to speak of him ever again. I went looking for him once. She smacked me." Charlotte tried to swallow the old hurt. Her throat stung. It never got easier. "I dreamed of him every night. Of a new life. A different me."

His gaze was unfathomable. At least now he knew the truth.

"But I'm not different. I'm *Charlotte the harlot*, bastard daughter of a common courtesan. And now you're saddled with me, too."

He took her hand. Refused to let her jerk free. "Look at me. What are you afraid of? That I'll reject you, too? That my association with you will ruin my pristine reputation? In case you've forgotten, I'm a hairsbreadth away from being tossed into debtors' prison." He forced her to meet his eyes. "I'm human, Charlotte. So are you. The circumstances of your birth are not your fault. How could I blame you for it?"

Hope dared to stir in her chest. Harsh reality tamped it down. She shook her head. "Others do. You can't change society. And what about your friends and family? What will they say when they discover you've wed the offspring of a whore?"

"My friends and family are no strangers to scandal." His tone was rueful, but his eyes held no trace of regret. "My sister married her husband the same week that she gave birth. One needn't have a head for figures to realize they must have taken a few liberties with the proper order of events. Sarah certainly won't judge you harshly. Nor do I."

Charlotte stared at him in amazement, scarcely able to comprehend his meaning. She had told him her darkest secrets, the very things she had spent a lifetime fighting to hide, and… it didn't change his view of her in the slightest?

She was human, he'd said without hesitation. Without realizing she'd struggled her entire life to be treated like a whole person. Her breath caught. She'd dreamed of society accepting her… but perhaps it was enough to be accepted by one man.

This man.

Still unable to believe he'd accepted her despite it all, she gave him a wobbly smile. He pulled her into his arms and just held her. Letting his strength comfort her. She hugged him tight. He would make a wonderful husband.

If only he weren't destined for gaol.

Chapter 10

Anthony cradled his sleeping bride in his arms as their hired hack rattled across the border into England. Charlotte had packed her valise without a word. There was nothing left for them in Scotland.

He had never been the sort of person who could sleep in a moving carriage, but he was not in the least surprised to see his wife succumb to her exhaustion. She had slept fitfully at best, after having realized her lifelong obsession with being reunited with her father had never been anything more than an impossible dream.

As for the confession that followed… Entering the parson's trap with a courtesan's daughter was perhaps not the most ideal of circumstances, but when had Anthony ever done the ideal thing? He could scarcely hold Charlotte accountable for something that had occurred prior to her birth.

Besides, Anthony was painfully cognizant of the

fact that he was no fine catch himself.

He had considered the situation over and over again—some might say dwelled upon the matter to the point of nausea. The only honorable way out of his scrape was to earn the owed sums himself.

The issue was how to buy more time.

London was the most viable city for easy employment. And the only place he could repay his debt, since Gideon's gaming parlor lay within city borders. But, given the new information about Charlotte, 'twas little wonder she had no interest in returning to a city that constantly made her feel worthless.

How could he sit behind a writing desk somewhere while his wife was suffering elsewhere? Yet he had to earn back the money, or risk leaving her even worse off than they were now.

At least they were heading south. On the move. His spirits brightened. Not just because they'd left the debt collector's ruffians behind, but because all of England still lay ahead.

London was not the only fashionable city. They could go to Bath. Perhaps there, Charlotte wouldn't be recognized or disparaged… And perhaps there, Anthony could scare up enough blunt to save his life—and his marriage.

He caressed the back of her hand.

She was so beautiful. So fragile, yet so strong. He longed to wrap his arms about her and keep her safe. Keep her *close*. He didn't want a marriage in name only. He wanted a union of hearts, of bodies. He wanted his Lady Luck to feel fortunate to have *him*. Wanted to prove that their marriage didn't need to be a mistake.

That their relationship didn't have to be temporary.

But now was not the moment to make promises about the future or take irreversible action. Neither of them was in a position to consummate a marriage whose future would come to an abrupt halt in less than a fortnight. But he *would* fix his mess. And once he deserved the title of husband, Charlotte would be his. Completely.

His throat dried. What if that day never happened? What if he managed to pay off his creditors and be the best man he'd ever been in his life, and it still wasn't enough? She hadn't chosen him. What if she would still prefer not to be wed to him, even if he did pay off his debts? He glanced over at Charlotte.

In his heart of hearts, he'd always dreamed his future wife would be a paragon. Not full of herself or high in the instep, but someone who was… complete without him. Someone who chose him because she *wanted* him, not because she was enamored by the baubles he bestowed upon her when he was flush.

If he did raise the blunt, what if Charlotte only stayed married to him because it was financially her best option, not because she loved him?

He swallowed. Did it matter anymore? Beggars could not be choosers. He had no particularly redeemable qualities, which left spoiling his loved ones when his pockets were flush his only option.

But if he focused on raising funds solely to stay out of gaol and keep his wife, he'd be teaching her to value him solely for money—just like he'd done with his nephews.

So what was he meant to do with Charlotte? How

could he appeal to her heart so that she would want to stay with *him*, rather than his money… or merely to salvage her reputation from the stigma of divorce?

He drummed his fingers against the carriage squab in frustration. Besides a father, the thing she wanted most was societal approbation—and he couldn't give it to her. No one could. She would never be accepted at high society gatherings, much less be granted an Almack's voucher to mingle with the crème de la crème. Even he couldn't do that.

She could probably be accepted into the societal fast set—rakes and gamblers and courtesans—but although Charlotte could move in those circles more freely, scandalous company wasn't what she desired. The gossiped-about set wasn't where she would wish to belong, or who she wanted to be.

But she had no other choice. Even now.

He lightly stroked her forearm. Having grown up along the fringes of the *beau monde* with both his parents, he could not imagine what it must be like to have been born a bastard. A man in such a position could still become a charming dandy or a famous poet or a respected officer in the army, but what was a woman to do? Especially when her face was recognizable as the very mirror of a known courtesan's.

Charlotte had never had a chance.

Anthony, on the other hand, did have a chance. He set his jaw. This was his opportunity not only to make something of himself—ideally something other than a Marshalsea prisoner—and, in doing so, give Charlotte a chance at an alternate future. A better one. Without the chains of the past.

A flutter of hope stirred in his belly. Once he paid off his debt, they could go anywhere. For the first time, it seemed that perhaps he might have something to offer besides money. He pressed his lips to her hair. To Charlotte, happiness stemmed from other sources. Peace. Safety. Love.

He couldn't change society to fit her dreams, but he could give her respect and worth in the sanctity of their home. Wherever that might be.

Starting here. Starting now.

Chapter 11

When they reached Newcastle upon Tyne that evening, Anthony found a comfortable inn in which to settle his exhausted wife, whilst he took a turn about the common areas in search of a moment's entertainment.

As anticipated, there was plenty to distract him.

A handful of couples were just setting out for some sort of local assembly with drink and dancing. A few younger bachelors joined the party in the hopes of encountering a nice young lady… or a naughty one, as the case might be. Assemblies had something for everyone.

The rest of the unattached gentlemen gathered in the inn's main salon. In moments, drinks were in every hand and the cozy chairs were rearranged into gaming areas.

Anthony's blood raced at the sight. How he had missed this! There was nothing he liked better than the thrill of a good wager. The risk of losing it all followed by a dizzying rush of euphoria when an improbable card won it all. This was where he thrived.

A few nights of exceptional hands, and he could come close to paying his debts back. It was unlikely, perhaps, but certainly not impossible. He'd almost done it in Scotland, had he not?

Before Charlotte had joined the table, he'd been well on his way to winning back at least a tenth of what he owed. If he could have a run like that every day for a fortnight, he'd not only pay off his debts, but he'd also have plenty left over to whisk Charlotte wherever she wished. Then he'd certainly be a husband she could be proud of.

And yet…

"Fairfax?" exclaimed a surprised voice from the other side of the room.

Anthony whirled to see a familiar face. "Thomas Quinton!"

"As I live and breathe." Quinton stared as if he couldn't quite credit his own eyes. "Daresay I've never seen you anywhere but St. James. What on earth brings you to Newcastle upon Tyne?"

Fleeing creditors seemed the wrong response if Anthony sought an opportunity to rid his friend of his purse at the tables. Instead he hedged with, "My wife wanted to visit family."

"Your *what?*" Quinton's jaw dropped. "Now you *must* be bamming me. Sit, sit. Allow me to buy you a drink while you regale me with lies about some poor debutante silly enough to tie the knot with a man who's never home at night." He laughed uproariously.

Anthony did not. Not because it was an inaccurate description of him—what single gentleman spent his evenings at home?—but because of the unflattering implication that Anthony was unlikely to change, even for a wife. Which wasn't at all true.

Was it? Guilt assailed him. He averted his eyes from the crowded card tables.

"All that's over," Anthony said firmly, needing it to be true. "I haven't abandoned my wife. She's recovering from a long journey. I don't see any harm in taking a stroll about in the meantime, do you?"

"Oh, perambulate all you like—be my guest! Just make sure you end up at my table, so you can tell me all about the bewitching creature you've hidden away upstairs. What's her name? Do I know her?"

"You don't," Anthony said quickly. "And the bewitching creature is Mrs. Fairfax to you."

"My, my, someone is prickly," Quinton teased. "Don't be the jealous sort, Fairfax. Every man enjoys a pretty face."

Anthony's shoulders stiffened, but not for the reasons Quinton believed. Anthony curled his fingers. What if the man recognized Charlotte? He didn't *think* Quinton would insult her, at least not purposefully, but a jokester like him could make just the right comment in front of just the wrong person, and even the briefest of stays at this inn would feel like a lifetime of misery to Charlotte.

His palms went clammy. If it was happening already, this far north, what would it be like the closer they got to London? How could he protect her from that? Even if they moved to Bath, they wouldn't escape the London crowd.

"Well?" Quinton took a seat at a gambling table and motioned toward the last empty chair. "Will you not join us?"

Anthony paused, tempted to join in. God knew he needed a win. Quinton's pockets weren't light, and if Anthony managed to sweep the table…

No. It was a bad idea. A wonderful, terrible, seductive idea. That he absolutely must not indulge. No matter how tempting it was. Or how quickly he could get them both out of this scrape, if luck would only be on his side.

His heart sped. No. He could not succumb. If not for himself, then for Charlotte. Aside from never forgiving him if he lost more money, his dwindling purse was upstairs in Charlotte's valise. Where it needed to stay. He wouldn't wake her. She needed to rest.

And Anthony needed to not lose what little they still had.

"No." He forced the words from his mouth. "I will not be joining you this time."

"What?" Quinton gasped, clutching his chest in melodrama. "Anthony Fairfax not wager? There can be only one reason. Sit, man. If you're at Point Non Plus, I'll give you ten quid to get you started." He turned to the other gentlemen at the gaming table. "Mind your purses. Fairfax can turn ten quid into two hundred faster than you can blink."

Anthony's pulse leapt, and he hesitated. Perhaps Quinton was right. With a few quid—even with a humble sovereign—Anthony had been known to turn a table to his advantage with devastating ease.

He'd also been known to lose the whole lot on the turn of a single card.

The empty chair beckoned him. He stared at the inviting stacks of ivory betting fish next to each fat purse. At the seductive fan of cards just waiting for him to pick them up and turn the table into a battleground. The pull was overwhelming.

His gaze darted about the room in search of escape. He couldn't sit down. Not even for a moment. One peek at those cards, the mere scent of a winning streak, and he'd wager every penny in his possession, right down to his buttons. He couldn't dare. Risking his own future was one thing. He would not risk Charlotte's.

He forced himself to bow. "I've a beautiful creature waiting for me, I'm afraid. Some other time, perhaps."

His fingers were shaking at the thought of walking away. At the urge to pick up the cards, the suspense at what their faces might show. At the delirious uncertainty of each new hand, and the accompanying rush of excitement thudding through his veins.

But gambling money he couldn't afford to lose was something a useless wastrel did—which was something he was no longer willing to be.

Charlotte, he reminded himself. He had to be a better man for Charlotte.

"Why, I cannot trust my eyes," Quinton exclaimed with an expression of honest shock. "If I try to tell anyone back home that Fairfax here turned down a game of cards, they'll laugh me right out of the club."

Frankly, Anthony couldn't believe it either.

Before his itchy gambling fingers could change his mind, he bid the company farewell and hurried out of the common area and back up to their chamber.

When he opened the door, Charlotte was out of bed and standing before the dressing table. His breath caught.

Ever since she'd stopped wearing the graying cosmetics, her beauty almost hurt to look at. She dazzled everyone who glimpsed her. Especially her husband. Sometimes Anthony found it difficult to believe that his current predicament was bad luck at all.

Not when it had given him Charlotte.

"Did you have supper?" she asked as she freshened her hair.

He shook his head. "I was waiting for you. Are you hungry?"

With a frown, she set down her pins and turned to face him. "You look pale. Did something happen?"

He touched his face, surprised she had discerned his conflicted emotions. The spinning of his head must be more visible from the outside than he'd supposed.

"Something *didn't* happen," he admitted. His addicted mind was still down at that gaming table. His fingers still longed for a quick game. He took a deep breath. "I didn't gamble."

She tilted her head as she considered his words.

He tensed. She had every reason not to believe him. The first impression he'd given was of winning everyone's money within minutes of making her acquaintance—and losing it all the very next instant.

She had every reason not to believe him. If Quinton couldn't believe Anthony would turn down the chance to win a few purses… He could hardly expect Charlotte to have any greater faith in him.

She returned to pinning her golden locks, her expression still inscrutable. "Well, that's good. One never knows if one will win or lose. You made the right choice."

Air escaped Anthony's lungs his lungs in a whoosh. He hadn't realized he'd been holding his breath. His head swam. He straightened his shoulders in preparation for much-deserved recriminations for the abominable choices he'd made in the past.

None came.

His mouth parted in shock. That was it? He stared at her as she finished dressing her hair. The first time he'd turned down a gaming table in fifteen years, the first time he realized he was strong enough to walk away, and when this fantastical event occurred… Charlotte simply believed he'd done the right thing without question. For some reason, she believed *in* him.

He strode across the room, cupped her face in his hands, and kissed her as if he could drink in her words, drown in her faith, die in her arms. Perhaps he could. She was his talisman.

In her eyes, he was a different man. A better man. With her lips pressed against his, he could almost imagine it was true. Wish it were. He cherished this moment.

She would never understand how much her trust and acceptance affected him. How much he'd needed it. How much he needed *her*. To have her melt into his embrace. To make her proud. To hold her close.

His heart thumped. He'd never been dependable

enough before for anyone to have a reason to believe in him. Even if her faith in him was in part because she hadn't known him long enough to understand the catastrophic depths of his unreliable nature, that innocence made him all the more determined never to fail her.

When she looked at him, she didn't see the man he was, but rather the man he *could* be.

The man he *would* be from this day forward. For her.

Chapter 12

Charlotte rubbed her tired eyes and gazed across yet another breakfast room in yet another inn. Leeds. Now they were in Leeds.

Every day brought them inexorably closer to London. Closer to the past she was desperate to forget. Closer to Anthony spending the rest of his future in debtors' gaol.

She would rather never return at all. She had no fond memories of England. Beau Brummell had fled to France to escape his creditors. To Charlotte, life in France didn't sound half bad. Anthony could avoid prison and she could avoid everyone who knew her past. They could present themselves as a perfectly respectable country couple. With no particular pretensions to grandeur and nary a sordid scandal in their completely fictional history.

To her, it sounded like heaven. But to Anthony, hell.

He had family in London. Friends all over England. People who cared about him, who respected him, who missed him. How lucky he was! If that were Charlotte's life, she would *never* leave. So how could she expect Anthony to?

"Mrs. Fairfax?" came a breathless voice from beside the breakfast table.

Charlotte glanced up and coaxed her weary face to smile at the elderly widow who'd spent the previous evening pouring her fears out to Charlotte over several cups of tea.

"How do you do this morning, Mrs. Rowden?" she asked. "Is something amiss?"

"Quite the opposite." Mrs. Rowden clasped her liver-spotted hands together and beamed at Charlotte. "Thank you so much for allowing me to bend your ear last night. Your advice was right on the mark. Before I retired for the night, I sent my son a letter informing him of my presence."

This time, Charlotte's smile was genuine. "I am so pleased to hear it. Uncertainty is one of the worst emotions to suffer. You've taken action, and soon you'll know. I do hope he accepts your apology."

"As do I." Mrs. Rowden wrung her hands. "Oh, how I'd love to meet my grandchildren. How big they must be by now!"

After chatting with Mrs. Rowden, Charlotte left the breakfast room and returned to her bedchamber to pack the valises.

Anthony had been out somewhere since well before dawn, hoping to earn a few coins doing this or that. She couldn't help but be proud of his efforts. Despite it all.

So far, he'd managed to earn more than enough to cover their travel expenses, but even with the contents of the purses they'd won in Scotland, their funds were meager compared to the size of his debt.

Yet he refused to give up.

It was incomprehensible. Noble. She hated that it was destined to fail. Hated that she couldn't stop herself from caring far too much.

She had to struggle to keep her shield intact so that she would not be destroyed if she lost him. He was the one person who unfailingly treated her as if she mattered. No matter how determinedly she reinforced her defenses, the walls crumbled a bit more every day. With him, happiness was no longer an illusion. He made her believe it was within her grasp… if only they could be assured of a future together.

She was just latching her trunk when a key turned in the door.

Anthony stepped into the room.

She grinned at him like a smitten halfwit. She couldn't help herself.

His chestnut hair was damp with sweat. His fancy clothes badly wrinkled. But the look of peace, of satisfaction, on his exhausted countenance as he handed her a trio of gold sovereigns made him as beautiful as an angel.

"How was it?" she asked.

"Wonderful," he answered without hesitation.

Her lips twitched. *Wonderful* was his reply every time she inquired. After a lifetime of living inside the hopelessness of her own mind, his boundless positivity was fast becoming one of her favorite traits.

Nothing bothered him for long. Not his creditors, not jarring hackney rides, not grass stains on expensive breeches. Not even the ignominy of having a light-skirt's illegitimate child for a wife.

When she was with him, sometimes she forgot her past altogether.

He dipped a handkerchief in the basin and blotted his forehead. "Do I have time to ring for a bath? What time did you reserve a hack?"

"I have already summoned a bath. The hackney will arrive within the hour."

His grateful expression filled her with warmth. She enjoyed doing her part. They had to make the most of however much time they would have together.

A knock on the door indicated the innkeeper had noted Anthony's return and had sent servants with a tub and steaming water. They set up the bath on the opposite side of a folding screen and assisted Anthony with a shave and the rest of his toilette.

Not for the first time, Charlotte was grateful for the presence of servants. The thought of her handsome husband nude… *No.* She would not think of such things. Not yet. If she allowed herself to take even a step down that path, losing him to Marshalsea prison would rip her soul to shreds.

Life had taken too much from her already for her to willingly let Fate rip a lover from her, too. Especially if it meant losing Anthony.

"I saw you holding court in the common area last night," he called from the other side of the privacy screen. "Have you given more thought to taking their money?"

She winced at the indiscretion. Servants were still in the room. Listening.

"Charging for your time, I mean," Anthony clarified.

She knew what he meant. And now, so did the footmen freshening his bathwater. Charlotte sighed. She doubted Anthony even registered their presence. She, on the other hand, knew all too well what it was like to be invisible. For everyone's sake, private matters were best left private.

"Can we discuss this later?" she called back.

"If you're worried about trade not being good ton," he continued blithely, "you're not ton and you never will be. Try to be practical."

She gritted her teeth. His honest words stung. She knew she would never be high society. She just wanted to be a member of *regular* society. To not give anyone any other reasons to look down their noses at her and judge her. Her nails bit into her palms. Even the footmen tending to Anthony's bathwater now knew not to mistake her for someone respectable.

Rather than open her heart in front of servants feigning deafness to the one-sided conversation, Charlotte threw herself diagonally across the mattress and closed her eyes to calm the familiar wave of embarrassment and powerlessness. *Deep breath in. Slowly let it out.* She blocked out Anthony's opinions and the sound of bathwater and instead concentrated on relaxing her toes inside her tightly laced half-boots. Then her ankles. Then her legs.

She imagined herself floating weightless as a cloud as each section of her body relaxed into nothingness. Her shoulders. Her neck. Now even her cares could slip away one by one, until all that was left was peace.

When she opened her eyes, the bath and the servants were gone and Anthony was at the mirror, folding his neck cloth.

He glanced at her in the looking glass. "Were you asleep?"

"No." She sat up and re-pinned a stray hair. "I just… turned off my senses for a bit. It helps when I need to relax. Or escape."

His forehead creased. "Turned off your senses? Which one? Sight?"

She shrugged. "Sight, sound, sensation. All of them."

He turned to stare at her. "You can do that?"

She set down her pins. He was right. She would never blend with society. She and the *beau monde* could never view their world through the same eyes.

"When I was young, my mother taught me to do it." It was not a memory she enjoyed revisiting. "At first, I thought she invented the technique to keep me quiet and calm while she entertained her… guests. Sometimes there were sounds no mother would wish her daughter to overhear."

Anthony paled. His voice softened. "And then?"

"Then one day, I was old enough to understand what the sounds meant. That some of my mother's lovers treated her like a duchess while others… did not." Her voice wobbled as she tried to staunch the memories. It didn't work. "I realized the relaxation technique was a strategy she used to survive. When she had no choice but to close off her emotions, her hearing, her sensation, and try to live through another night. Another hour."

Anthony's expression was horrified.

To Charlotte, it was just life. One learned to live with the horror. Somehow.

"Her relaxation technique was the most helpful gift she ever gave me." She gave a crooked smile despite the lump in her throat. "Closing myself off has often been the one thing that has helped me survive."

He rushed to the bed and pulled her into his arms. He stroked her hair as he held her close. "You don't have to shut yourself off anymore. Now you have me. We'll fight the world together."

If only that were true. Her eyes pricked. She did not have him. He was the reason she'd needed to retreat inward.

She didn't relax into the warmth of his embrace. He would be gone in little over a week. His supportive presence was ephemeral, his affection a temporary salve to a lifetime of wounds.

The idea of him—the intoxicating fantasy of being loved, or even cared about, now and forever—was the precise lie she needed to protect her scarred heart against. These days in his company had been the closest to "normal" life she'd ever experienced. She longed to believe it could last. But there was no denying the truth. They had less than a week left.

A knock sounded upon the door. "Mrs. Fairfax? Your hackney is here."

Grateful for the interruption, she sprang out of

Anthony's arms to open the door. A pair of footmen lifted their luggage and hefted it out to the street.

Charlotte hurried to follow.

Anthony reached her side in an instant. He placed her hand on his arm, but asked no further questions. Made no hopeful promises. Perhaps he didn't have any.

Or perhaps he'd realized some truths were better left unspoken.

As they crossed the common area toward the exit, footsteps rushed up from behind them and a strong hand nearly jerked Charlotte's arm from its socket. She spun about in alarm.

A wild-eyed Mrs. Rowden stood before her, tears streaming down her face.

"Mrs. Fairfax… Oh, Mrs. *Fairfax*." The widow swiped at her cheeks.

Charlotte's heart twisted. The poor woman must have received terrible news. But no matter what the outcome, Charlotte's advice had been sound. Once Mrs. Rowden knew where she stood with her family, she could finally move on. "Your son responded to your letter?"

"Tea," she whispered, as if that single syllable held all the power of the universe. Her breaths hitched. "He's invited me for tea, this very afternoon. It's not an invitation to stay overnight, much less to spend a few weeks with them—but it is more than I dreamed. My *grandchildren* will be there. I'll finally get to meet them."

Joy coursed through Charlotte's tense muscles. "That is marvelous. I was worried about you. I'm glad we ran into each other again so that you could let me know."

"I don't just want to tell you. I want to *thank* you." Mrs. Rowden fumbled for her reticule and thrust the banknotes therein into Charlotte's hand. "Money doesn't begin to repay your kindness. You've given me my life back. You've given me my son's life, and my grandchildren's lives. Bless you, child. I will never be able to thank you enough."

"I…" Words failed her.

"Thank you again." Mrs. Rowden gave Charlotte a warm embrace. "I wish you Godspeed."

Charlotte's head was topsy-turvy as the older woman rushed off to prepare herself for her tea. Mrs. Rowden credited Charlotte with reuniting her family. And had *hugged* her in thanks. In front of witnesses!

"That was incredible," she mouthed as Anthony helped her into the coach and climbed in beside her. She still couldn't quite comprehend what had just happened.

He rescued the banknotes from her trembling fingers.

"I'll be damned," he breathed in obvious shock. "She gave you twenty pounds!"

Charlotte hadn't even thought of the money. She was still floating at the experience of being seen. Remembered. Appreciated. Mrs. Rowden had not just sung Charlotte's praises—she'd acknowledged her publicly, in front of everyone. She'd treated Charlotte like an equal.

"Twenty pounds," Anthony repeated, his wide eyes stunned. "For one piece of advice."

His words punctured Charlotte's fog of pleasure. She seized the notes from his hand to count them herself.

Eighteen… nineteen… twenty. Her mouth fell open. She clutched the bills to her chest. Mrs. Rowden had given her twenty pounds for helping her reunite with her son.

As the jarvey set the hack in motion, Charlotte stared out the window in a state of unreality. Her mind bubbled with dizzy joy. Twenty pounds was as much as Anthony could earn doing odd tasks for an entire week. He was right. Counseling wealthy people was more than profitable. It was astonishing. Hope wriggled into her heart.

What if she could pay off Anthony's debt?

He didn't want her money, said his vowels were his responsibility—plus their current finances couldn't come close to resolving the matter—but what if *she* could? Perhaps not today, perhaps not in a fortnight, but even if the creditors took him away… she might still get him back.

Then, once he had his freedom, she could talk him into staying as far away from London as possible.

Chapter 13

By the time their hired conveyance pulled into Nottingham, Charlotte's bones were exhausted from so many days of travel. Scotland seemed like a century ago.

Her heart, however, was yearning to hope again. Not in a childhood dream of a long-lost father who would sweep her into a new life, but in the flesh-and-blood man seated next to her in the carriage. Anthony's unshakeable faith that good fortune was always right around the corner was baffling, but infectious. Perhaps this time luck would find them both.

She tried to be cautious, tried to fight the unexpected sense of comfort she felt in his presence. It couldn't last. Yet she wished it could.

Impulsively, she turned to hold his strong, handsome face in her hands and pressed her lips to his as if this might be their last chance. He cupped the back of her head as he responded in kind, his mouth as hungry as her own. She let him hold her close. There was nowhere else she preferred to be than in his embrace.

One by one, she extinguished every sense except for their kiss. The clatter of the carriage disappeared until all she could hear was the beating of her heart. The jarring bounce of stiff wheels over uneven road vanished, as did the chill of the night air whistling through the carriage door. All she felt was the strength in his arms, the heat of his embrace. The dizzying taste of his mouth covering hers.

Another woman might wish such a kiss would never stop. Not Charlotte. She hoped it would occur again and again. That her future would be filled with a thousand passionate kisses, safe in the arms of this man.

His presence would always make her feel as though she'd slipped into a dream. A place where she was the thing that mattered most. Where every kiss was a promise of five more to come.

She would never take him for granted. Charlotte didn't pull away until her lungs were out of breath and her heart was in grave danger of surrendering itself completely.

Anthony stared at her, his eyes heavy-lidded with arousal. His slow smile was as dazed as her own. "What was that for? Tell me, so I can be sure to do it again."

"For being you." She could tell he didn't believe her, but the truth was both as simple and as alarming as that. He was such a joy to be around. Easy to talk to, easy to travel with, easy to kiss until every beat of her heart pulsed with his name.

"Nottingham," the jarvey called out. "Shall I take

a few laps about the square, or do you want to go straight to an inn?"

Cheeks burning, she jerked back to the other side of the carriage and tried to arrange herself as demurely as possible.

Anthony's eyes met hers. "Definitely the inn."

She tried to slant him a quelling look, but ended up smiling back at him instead. With Anthony, there was never a reason for shame or embarrassment. Every moment was simply part of the adventure they were building together.

"Any specific inn?" the jarvey asked. "There's three up ahead."

Anthony glanced out of the window and feigned deep thought. He tilted his head toward Charlotte. "Are you in a White Lion sort of humor or are you feeling a bit more Haystack and Horseshoe today?"

"With a full moon tonight?" she teased back. "Only a white lion can protect us."

"The lady has chosen the second inn on the left," Anthony informed the driver.

As the jarvey steered his horses in front of the White Lion, another carriage pulled to a stop a few yards behind them.

"Popular choice." Anthony smiled at Charlotte in approval. "Must be a wise decision."

Popular. Her earlier elation faded at the idea of staying somewhere fashionable enough that she was likely to be recognized. She might have just ruined the adventure.

Although she'd tried her hardest to stay out of sight, sharing a face with a courtesan made attempts at anonymity laughable.

Most men of a certain set knew who her mother was. Many of them, intimately. "Gentlemen" with presumptuous comments and shameless leers were the best of the lot. Others simply assumed "like mother, like daughter," and yanked her into the nearest shadow with every expectation of enjoying a quick tup.

It was embarrassing, infuriating, and demeaning. And it would be all the worse when it happened in front of Anthony. He still saw her as a respectable woman. As a *person.*

She didn't want to change his mind.

As he handed her down from the carriage, a short man with a limp and a scuffed black beaver hat alighted from the coach that had pulled up behind them.

She frowned. Not *a* man. The same man with a limp she'd seen at the inn back in Scotland. Her stomach hollowed.

For the man in the scuffed hat to show up at the same randomly selected inn, two hundred miles south, having matched their grueling breakneck pace… It was more than an improbable coincidence. Her skin went cold.

They were being followed.

"Anthony," she hissed, then stepped in front of him to block the approaching gentleman's view. Her heart thundered. "The debt collectors have found us."

"I'll handle it." He eased in front of her, stepping directly into harm's way. His voice lowered when he caught sight of the man. "Was that gentleman one of the other guests at the Kitty and Cock Inn?"

"Yes," she whispered back. "Should we run for it?

Our luggage is still in the hackney."

He shook his head slowly in confusion. "That's not one of the enforcers."

She blinked. "Then who is it?"

"Dashed if I know." Anthony's eyes narrowed. "But he's coming this way."

She wrapped her arms about her chest and tried not to panic.

"Excuse me, miss?" the man called out.

Anthony stepped forward. "She is my wife."

"Ma'am," the man corrected. He bowed in haste. "Sir, could I speak to your wife for a moment? Alone?"

Dread sent her a step back. Who was this presumptuous man? A client of her mother's? He couldn't possibly mean to insult her beneath her husband's nose, could he?

Anthony crossed his arms. "I'm not leaving her side."

The man cleared his throat. "Ma'am, I couldn't help but notice the distinctive ruby earrings you were wearing at the Kitty and Cock Inn. Do you mind telling me how they came to be in your possession?"

Her stomach turned at the unspoken implication. He thought she'd *stolen* them? The irony heated her cheeks. She'd worn the rubies so her father would recognize her… and instead, had labeled herself as a thief.

"He has no claim to your jewelry," Anthony murmured into her ear. "You don't have to answer."

But of course she did. People like her never stopped having to defend themselves against insinuation and accusation.

"They were my mother's," she blurted. "And before that, my father's. I think."

The man's blank expression did not change. "I see. Who is your father, ma'am?"

Her throat closed. She could not answer. There was nothing to say.

"Never mind him, Charlotte," Anthony murmured again. "He's no one."

It was too late. All her newfound self-assurance had already fled, leaving her shoulders as deflated as her confidence.

Very well. If this man had come all the way from Scotland to accuse her of something, he must have had a reason. It was better to deal with suspicion before it had the opportunity to spiral even more out of control.

"I don't know who my father is," she answered quietly, unable to meet the man's eyes. "There's no way to tell."

"As it happens, ma'am…" He lowered his hat. "That's not precisely true."

Her startled gaze jerked up.

"Who *are* you?" Anthony snarled.

"Mr. Ralph Underwood, Esquire. One of the Duke of Courteland's solicitors and a trusted advisor." The man gestured at Charlotte. "And this is His Grace's daughter."

She gaped at the strange man in disbelief, then burst out laughing at such a ridiculous mistake. "I can assure you, my birth had no such noble beginnings. You have me confused with someone far more fortunate than I."

"The set you were wearing," the solicitor continued, "has belonged to the Courteland family for several generations. Now that I've had a closer look, I am certain. Those jewels are part of a collection that includes not just a necklace and earrings, but also a matching bracelet and tiara. The latter two pieces remain at the Courteland country estate."

This… wasn't a mistake?

"I don't understand," Charlotte stammered. "Perhaps the rubies were once part of a set, but I cannot possibly be related to a duke. My mother…"

The solicitor withdrew a folded parchment from a pocket inside his greatcoat and studied the cramped handwriting covering one side. "Are you the sole offspring of one Judith Devon, of London?"

"Yes," she croaked through a suddenly raspy throat.

She had been born with the stigma of her mother's profession, but she would not deny their connection. Up until last week, her mother was all Charlotte had ever had.

"In that case, I am in possession of a document signed by His Grace's own hand, indicating you are indeed his daughter."

His Grace's daughter? Charlotte sagged backwards against Anthony. A duke. Signed by his own hand. She tried to process the solicitor's claim.

Her father wasn't a *laird*. He was a *lord*. Her child's mind had muddled the two, and her mother had never corrected the mistake—she'd simply added to his legend.

"Not Scotland," she whispered in stupefaction.

"*Courteland.*"

Her mind was spinning.

She might still be a courtesan's by-blow, but she wasn't merely one of many such unfortunate bastard children. She was the daughter of a duke. One who *recognized* her. In writing! She grabbed Anthony's hands, giddy with joy. He grinned back at her.

"I have a father," she choked out, half laughing, half crying. The world was so much brighter than it had been mere moments before. "Anthony, I have a *father*!"

"Actually, ma'am… I'm afraid you—you *had* one." The solicitor cleared his throat. "A few weeks ago, His Grace passed away, at his London home."

An icy breeze whipped straight through Charlotte's heart, ripping away every trace of the joy she should have known better than to believe in. Of course she would never meet him. Girls like her didn't get to have fathers. Not even for a moment. A great hollow void spread through her, replacing her excitement with devastation.

Her father had known who she was. Had known that he had sired her. Worse, as a member of the House of Lords, he'd lived at least half the year in London. *Every* year. An hour's journey at the most from where a scared, lonely little girl rocked herself every night on her bedchamber floor, staring at her locked door and dreaming of a different life. Of a father who could whisk her away from the fear and the self-loathing and the endless humiliations.

As it turned out, her father *could* have whisked her away. Or taken her out for ices. Or visited her, just once. Something. *Anything.*

It would've meant the world to her.

And now he was dead. Now that she finally knew who he was, finally knew where to find him, she would never get to meet him. Never spend a single moment in his presence.

Not because she was too late. But because he hadn't cared enough to bother, back when he still had time.

"Why are you telling me this?" she asked dully. As if every word, every breath, didn't rake open all the old scars guarding her heart. "I never knew him. He's dead. Nothing matters anymore."

The solicitor coughed. "Actually, ma'am…"

Realization hit her.

"Do his real children want the jewels back?" Of course they did. They were the important ones. The children who mattered. She tore open her reticule, shoved the necklace at Anthony, and the earrings.

"Sell them back for as high a price as you can get," she gasped, hated how, even now, relinquishing the jewels felt like carving off the most important part of her. "And keep the money. Those stones mean nothing. I can't bear for them to touch my skin."

Anthony put his arm around her and held her close.

The solicitor cleared his throat. "Ma'am, you needn't surrender the rubies. At least, not yet. But your presence is required at the Courteland house in Mayfair one week from today for the reading of his will. Next Tuesday, at one o'clock sharp."

She stared at him uncomprehendingly. "For the…

what?"

"Until the bequests are read, I have no way to know if His Grace has settled a sum upon you, or a bit of land, or perhaps the other ruby pieces to complete the set. But as a named party in the will, I'd like to offer you my services to help manage any windfall you might receive." He touched his lapel. "For a fee, of course."

She was too drained of all humor to laugh even halfheartedly at the solicitor's blatant mercenariness. The man had shown up out of nowhere, had given her more joy, more tangible reasons to believe in her future, than she'd ever had in her life—then immediately destroyed every hope he'd just helped to sow. And now he wanted part of whatever her father had left her?

Or worse, what if he was lying?

"How did you find me?" She didn't bother to hide the suspicion from her voice.

The solicitor had the grace to look somewhat abashed. "I glimpsed the rubies when you were dining at a posting house across the Scottish border and was convinced they were Courteland's. But I had to be certain. I waited until I saw you only wear the earrings, not the necklace, and I sneaked into your chamber to confirm my suspicions."

"You broke into my chamber?" Fury exploded from her chest. "How *dare* you!"

He lifted a shoulder. "I had to know for certain. What if they weren't the same jewels? What if you weren't his daughter?"

"What if I had bashed in your head with a fire iron?" Anthony growled.

"My duty is to His Grace's dukedom." The solicitor lifted his nose. "What if the family jewels had fallen into the hands of someone without Courteland blood?"

"Heaven forbid," she said sarcastically.

Damn the pompous solicitor. And damn her father for not caring about his daughter until he was already in his grave.

"Be advised that His Grace is unlikely to have left you anything substantive," the solicitor warned her. "Illegitimate children are unseemly for a duke. But in the event he bequeathed you something of value… I am at your service."

For a fee. Charlotte's fingernails dug into her palms. To the devil with the duke and his solicitor both. *She* didn't even want whatever her father had left her. The only reason she was still listening was in case she could help Anthony. To get the best price for the rubies, they would have to go to London. And she would have to withstand the inevitable snubs and degradation that came with it.

"Here's the address." The solicitor handed her an array of papers. "And a contract, should you desire my aid. You will see that your interests will be well protected from your family, from solicitors—perhaps even from your own husband, should you wish. You need only to sign the document and I will represent you."

"That will do," Anthony snapped. He wrapped his arm about Charlotte's shoulders. "I believe you've helped enough for one day."

Her chest wouldn't stop pounding. She stumbled

when she tried to walk away. Her mind was too full of regret and yearning. Too focused on the father she could have had… if she had but known his name years ago.

The solicitor tipped his hat and turned away, then paused to glance back over his shoulder at Charlotte. "Oh, and ma'am… I'm sorry for your loss."

A half laugh, half sob ripped up from her heart and tangled in her throat. Such false words. No one was sorrier for her loss than Charlotte. The loss of her father. The loss of opportunity. The loss of her dreams.

The loss of her belief that, if her father had only known she existed, he might have loved her enough to save her.

Might have even saved them both.

Chapter 14

Anthony ushered Charlotte inside the posting house and away from Courteland's solicitor. Keeping a close eye on his wife, Anthony commissioned a room and coordinated the delivery of their luggage in order to get her into the privacy of a bedchamber as quickly as possible.

Charlotte stood woodenly by his side throughout. Not speaking, not making eye contact, not even changing expression. Walking where he led her. Remaining motionless when he did not. An empty shell.

Someone who didn't know her might assume her to be blind, deaf, and mute, so completely oblivious was she to everything around her.

Anthony made no such assumptions. He knew it was true. Her mother's so-called relaxation technique had become not just a defense mechanism, but Charlotte's best weapon against the outside world.

She had spent her life believing others didn't think

she mattered. Shutting them out was her way to show them they didn't matter to her, either. She didn't need their superiority, their insults, or their disgust. She didn't need the blackguard father who couldn't be bothered to spend a penny to clothe her or even spare a moment for a child he well knew he'd sired. She didn't need the world at all.

The problem was, Anthony was part of that world. By shutting out the grief and the pain and the longing, she had closed herself off from him, too. He wished he could be there with her, wherever she was. He wanted to help protect her. She didn't have to do it all alone. She could count on him, too. At least for this moment.

She just had to let him in.

He stoked the fire in the grate, then crossed to kneel before his wife. "Charlotte."

She didn't answer.

He took her hands. "I know it hurts. I shan't tell you not to let some egotistic jackanapes wound your feelings from beyond the grave, because I have never been in your position and I might well feel the same pain you do. But do not give your father more importance than he deserves. He's gone, Charlotte. I'm right here. He cannot hurt you anymore."

At least, Anthony hoped Courteland couldn't hurt her anymore. There was no telling what the will reading might bring. What if the other family members were cruel to her? He couldn't recall the Duke of Courteland having an heir apparent, but that wasn't necessarily a boon. Distant cousins fighting for scraps could be even more vicious than a half-sibling might be.

And while Anthony was here right now, holding her slender cold hands in his, would he still be there a week from now when she needed him? Dread washed over him. And fear. His debts were due prior to the reading of the will. By then, he might already be in Marshalsea.

Hands shaking, he helped her into her night rail and carried her to bed. After taking off his heavy boots and greatcoat, he curled in beside her, determined never to let her go.

Gently, he stroked her hair. He wasn't certain whether being named in Courteland's will would prove to be a blessing or a curse. After all this time, after never taking an interest in his daughter while he was still alive to do so, what the deuce would the blackguard have left her in his will? A bracelet? Land? A pittance?

Money would solve all the problem with his debts. But even if it were enough money to right his wrongs, he yearned to be as dependable as Charlotte needed him to be. To be responsible for a change. To provide for *her*, to clean up his own scrapes, to fix his life without ruining hers. To be a better man than her father.

Trepidation snaked down his spine. What if the creditors took whatever the old duke left Charlotte, and it still wasn't enough to keep Anthony out of prison? He could never forgive himself if his past actions robbed her of her inheritance, after everything she'd already lost.

He doubted Charlotte would ever forgive him either.

Chapter 15

Anthony awoke the following morning with Charlotte still cradled in his arms.

Gently, he kissed her forehead. He was glad that he could do at least this much for her. To be there when she needed someone. More than that—to be the one that she needed.

Even if he wasn't yet certain he would always be there, he could swear to never let her down for as long as he was able. He hoped it was for a long time.

It might be less than a week.

"Good morning." She opened her eyes and smiled up at him shyly. "Thank you for calming me last night. I feel much better."

He kissed the tip of her nose. "Good morning, yourself. Did you sleep well?"

"How could I not?" Her cheeks turned pink. "I was in your arms."

He grinned. "We should do this again some time."

"Every time." A shadow flickered across her face as if she too had just remembered they might not have much time left. "Today we head toward London?"

"Toward, yes. We should rest for the night near Northampton."

She pushed a golden curl from her face. "I feel as if all we do is ride in carriages and rest for the night."

"That *is* all we do." He stroked her cheek. "That, and I earn a bob or two sowing a few fields while you make twenty quid sipping tea with some wealthy old biddy."

She laughed and cuffed his chest. "Mrs. Rowden was a sweet lady."

"So sweet her own son didn't want to speak to her?"

"Do you speak to *your* parents?" she shot back.

"Not as often as I should," he admitted with a twinge. "I make certain to call every time the tables leave me flush, but Lady Fortune is not something one is capable of planning around."

"How delightful—blame the woman," she murmured with an arch look. "Lady Fortune isn't even real and she's responsible for everything."

"Lady Fortune," he informed her, "is right here in my arms."

"And much prefers the close view of pillow lines upon your face to the monotony of being in a carriage," she assured him.

He batted his eyelashes at her. "Your words… they're like poetry."

She nodded. "'Romantic poetess' shall be my reserve profession, should the current stream of wealthy old biddies come to an end."

He clutched his heart dramatically. "Let us pray for indecisive old biddies to fall from the sky like… wealthy drops of rain."

"You… should perchance not become a poet, either." She gave him a consoling pat. "I hope this does not crush your dreams."

"Not a chance. When I was young, I wanted to be a pirate." He chuckled in remembrance. "Or a botanist. I had very eclectic tastes."

Her eyes twinkled. "I imagine your parents had their own idea of suitable pursuits for a young man of your station."

He shrugged rather than respond. There was little to say. His parents never thought he'd be much of anything. *They* had never managed to match their income to their spending. Why would their son fare any better?

Nonetheless, they were always pleased to see him. And their contentment made him happy. "What do you think about paying a call on them when we get to London?"

Her lips parted in surprise. A flicker of fear marred her brow for a moment. Then a tentative smile curved her lips.

"That sounds delightful," she said shyly. Her eyes shone with hope. "I would love to meet your parents."

"I am certain they would be delighted to meet you, too," he answered automatically. He realized his mistake the moment her happy expression wilted.

"You know they won't." The shine in her eyes went dull. "They'll be disappointed in me. They'll be disappointed in you for marrying me."

"They will not be disappointed," he assured her. "Why should they? Have you not considered they mightn't have the slightest inkling of your past?"

"Have you not considered that they might?" An anguished expression filled her eyes. "What if your father takes one look at me and asks if I'm the daughter of Judith Devon, the courtesan? Perhaps they shared an 'understanding' a decade or two ago. Perhaps they still do. What then?"

He winced. That would be… awkward, at best.

"Even if all of that happens…" He cupped her cheek and forced her to meet his eyes. "*I* don't care if you came from the wrong side of the blanket or if you fell from the sky. Just focus on me, and what I like."

"Hmm." Her features softened. "What do you like?"

He smoothed a lock of hair away from her face. "I like this brilliant brain of yours, and I love how even perfect strangers are drawn to your compassion and logic." He kissed her forehead. "I like how they automatically respect your opinions, and I love how proud I am of you."

Her cheeks flushed scarlet. "My opinions mean nothing. It's just common sense."

He brushed his thumb along her cheekbone. "I like these gorgeous blue eyes because they can see which henwits have misplaced their common sense so you can try to help them. These eyes are also remarkably perceptive at a gaming table. If a gentleman doesn't mind his step, he might find himself losing more than his purse."

"Like when you offered me your 'purity?'" Her

tone was dry, but her eyes twinkled.

"A selfless sacrifice," he assured her. "To prove I was a gentleman."

She arched her eyebrows. "Was there any doubt?"

His heart warmed as the sparkle returned to her eyes. He leaned forward to kiss each corner of her mouth, then pressed a long kiss to the center of her lips. "I like this mouth because it hides a rapier wit. Perhaps 'hides' is the wrong term. I like this mouth because of the deep, grievous wounds each word makes as it cuts across my fragile ego like a—"

She burst out laughing. "I couldn't dent your fragile ego with an anvil."

"Fortuitously, we do not possess such an instrument, so we are spared the experiment." He lowered his head and gave her delicious mouth a kiss heated with sensual promise. He touched his lips to the soft line of her jaw, behind the lobe of her ear, down the curve of her neck. "I love your beautiful neck because even when you try to hide your interest in my kisses, the pulse at the base of your throat gives you away… as it's doing right now."

Her heartbeat fluttered against his lips, sending his blood racing. She was breathtaking. He tried to control his body's natural response. There would be other opportunities to indulge in his own release. This morning, he wanted to keep the focus on her. To give her pleasure.

She deserved no less.

Charlotte had been raised by a woman who had spent her life pleasing men. She had perhaps never been treated with respect and consideration. Her most likely future had always been to follow her mother's path. But that was no longer necessary. Now she had him.

He gave her a long, sweet kiss. This was a new life. She needed to know that her wants and desires not only mattered—for him, they came first. *She* came first. In the bedchamber and out of it.

He began a torturously slow series of soft, teasing kisses along the delicate line of her collarbone, across her chest, then up the plump curve of her breast above the bodice of her night rail. Heart pounding, he paused at the neckline and touched the tip of his tongue to her bare flesh.

Desire surged through him. He tried his best to tamp it down. His finances were nowhere near stable enough to consider making love. But there were other ways to bring her pleasure. He could at least offer that much.

Her nipples strained against the thin lawn of her night rail. He ached to dispense with the slow, tantalizing game and take her breast in his mouth. He had wanted her for so long.

Slowly, he allowed his parted lips to graze one of her taut nipples.

She gasped and arched into him. The delicious contact made the exquisite yearning for a deeper physical connection that much stronger. Flames of desire licked through his veins. He reminded himself to push back his own need and focus solely on hers. If nothing else, he could at least give her one perfect memory.

He hooked the tip of his finger beneath the bodice of her night rail. "May I?"

She nodded wordlessly, her eyes dark with passion. Did she no longer think it necessary to refrain from consummating their marriage? Or was she no longer thinking at all?

Anthony pushed away his doubt. This might be a terrible idea—but he needed to do it. To prove to her how important she had become to him. He wasn't going to take her choices away. He was going to give her pleasure.

She deserved it.

He tugged the hem of her night rail off her shoulders and below her breasts. His blood raced at the sight. She was beautiful. If she wanted him to stop, he would. But until then… Slowly, he lowered his mouth to her bare skin, reveling in the taste of each dip and curve, in her gasp as he suckled her nipple, in the gooseflesh on her skin as her body arched to meet him.

His breath caught. He loved how responsive she was. Her body was made for pleasure. His pulse thrummed as he slid his hand from the curve of her breasts down her flat stomach to her parted legs. He was consumed with the desire to possess her. Yet this moment was not for him, but for her. She was the center of his thoughts. Here, he could prove it.

Breathing ragged, he pushed the hem of her night rail up to her thighs and slid his hand beneath it.

She grabbed his wrist, her eyes wide. "What are you doing?"

He blinked. "Isn't it obvious what we're doing?"

"Why would it be obvious?" she stammered, then flushed as she took his meaning.

Realization dawned on him at the same moment.

Dear God. He had handled the moment all wrong. "You're a virgin?"

"You thought I was a *whore?*" Her eyes filled with shame and fury.

"No, I… I just assumed…" He ran a hand through his hair in frustration. Of course he hadn't believed her a whore—but nor would he have imagined her still a maiden. He had only meant to give her pleasure. Instead, he had insulted her.

Devil take it. His mistake had thoroughly ruined the moment—and quite possibly the peace they'd found in their relationship. He'd thought she wanted the same thing he did. Never would he have believed one day he would be shocked to discover his wife was a virgin.

"Your mother is a courtesan. You grew up in the same house in which she plied her trade. It seemed reasonable to assume you might have a certain level of…"

"Experience?" she demanded, eyes glassy with hurt. "I do not. Now you know."

He let go of her hem.

She shoved him away. One arm covering her bare chest, she lurched out of the bed and over to her valise, where she snatched up a mud-colored gown and marched behind the folding screen to don it.

He rolled onto his back and covered his eyes. Blast it all. He'd meant to make her feel better, not worse. To show her how much she mattered. Instead, he'd reinforced her belief that there was no escape from being judged by her mother's actions. Not even with him.

If someone who cared about her could hurt her so carelessly… How much worse would it be when they reached London, and other people began to put her in her place on purpose? And how much worse would it be if he was no longer there to protect her?

Chapter 16

Charlotte stood just outside the door of their last inn before London. Her legs shook. A hired hackney awaited them at the curb, its door flung wide and inviting.

She could not have wished to run away more.

London was going to be horrid. After last night, *anywhere* would be terrible. Her chest constricted with dread. She could resolve to keep a shield about herself all she wished, but the truth was Anthony was already in her heart.

And breaking it from the inside out.

This morning's misunderstanding was not wholly his fault. His assumptions about her chastity—or lack thereof—were identical to those of every other man she'd ever met. She'd just hoped, with him, it could be different. That he wouldn't view her as an extension of her mother.

Charlotte realized he might not have consciously

thought of her as a whore, as a prostitute who received coin in exchange for her favors. But he had seen her as easy pickings all the same. *You grew up in the same house in which she plied her trade.*

He had clearly been shocked to learn she was still a virgin. To him, why should she be? In his experience, a proper debutante guarded her maidenhead because it was the most valuable social currency she owned. Someone like Charlotte, on the other hand, possessed no social currency. A courtesan's illegitimate child would never be on the marriage mart. Her purity was meaningless.

Even the butcher's son, the street sweepers, saw in her only the opportunity for a quick, forgettable tup. The men she knew neither believed in her virginity nor cared in the slightest. They weren't going to marry her. They weren't even planning on asking her name.

And now Anthony. Wed to her. *Kind* to her. The closest she'd ever come to feeling as though she had somewhere she belonged. As an equal.

Yet once he knew the truth, even he had only seen her through the lens of what her mother had been.

Charlotte's chest tightened in despair.

He had once said his goal was to deserve her. She had always known she was the one who would never deserve him. Now they both knew. He couldn't help but identify her as a courtesan's daughter. To associate their bed-play with her knowledge of her mother's trade. But she had no wish to share her marriage bed with her mother's shadow.

If she wasn't even her own person with someone as kind as Anthony, what hope was there at all?

Perhaps it was simply human nature. After all, had she not done the same to him? Identify him as a selfish, self-important scoundrel because that was she had assumed all men like him would be? She swallowed thickly. How could she blame him for returning the favor? Why should she expect, or deserve, anything else?

She straightened her shoulders in determination. Nothing would make him forget her past. But she didn't want *whore's daughter* to be what he saw every time he looked at her. She was not her mother.

"Holding court" as an impromptu advisor in travelers' inns had made her realize she did have value. Her mind was just as important as her body. Thanks to Anthony, she was more of a complete person today than she had been before she met him.

If she wanted her husband to see her as more than the product of her past, she would have to show him her future. And her courage.

Even if that meant returning to London and facing the wrath and disgust of her father's real family. The ones that mattered.

He was dead. She would have to accept whatever role he wished to give her. Even if it was that of a mistake. Even if she was forced to return the rubies to their rightful home.

She stared straight ahead at the yawning maw of the hackney cab and tried not to run away. She was returning to that cursed city not for herself, but for her husband. London was where Anthony would have his best chance of prying himself out of his tight situation. That it would be as miserable as ever for her did not signify.

Now they were a team.

They would find a way to save him from debtors' prison. Somehow.

At that moment, Anthony stepped out of the inn. Despite a rather tense breakfast—after the morning's upset, she hadn't wished to speak to him until she'd had the opportunity to collect her thoughts—he nonetheless offered his arm without hesitation.

"Ready?" he asked.

Of course not. Taking a coach into London was like taking a hackney straight to hell. But if it helped him, the sacrifice would be worth it.

She gripped his arm. "Ready."

"I apologize for leaving your side for such a long moment," he said as he helped her into the carriage. "I ran into an old friend as I was settling the account and he would not cease nattering on about the latest Grenville musicale. Were you terribly bored in the tavern room?"

She shook her head. At this inn, at least, her face had become synonymous with a sympathetic ear. She was never alone for long.

"Before I stepped out of doors, I met a woman seeking to hire a new governess. Based on what I learned speaking to the one who was desperate to leave the children behind, I think I was able to offer the woman a few sound suggestions for questions to ask during the interview."

"I've no doubt your advice was on the mark." His eyes sparkled as he helped her into the carriage. "Was it another wealthy old biddy? Did she shower you with pound notes, too?"

"She offered to. She said I'd saved her hours of time and the wasted salary of hiring someone unlikely to stay."

His brow wrinkled in confusion. "Then why didn't you accept her money?"

"I wanted something else." Charlotte took a deep breath. *This* was the future she wanted him to see when he looked at her. She smiled hesitantly. "I told her my name was Mrs. Fairfax, and the best way she could repay me would be to tell all her friends to schedule a consultation any time they found themselves in need of an impartial confidante or good, sound advice."

His eyes widened with respect. "Darling, that's *brilliant.* Such a practical solution should cement you all the more as a woman wise beyond compare."

Charlotte's cheeks heated. She had never been called *darling* before. And had rarely been complimented. Today was full of firsts. Perhaps he did see her differently. "Those were almost precisely her words."

"Then she is an excellent judge of character." He brushed his thumb across her cheek in wonder. "Every day, I discover yet another reason to be amazed that you are mine."

Hope bubbled through her. Those were exactly the sort of words she'd dreamed of someday hearing. Pleasure warmed her cheeks as she gazed back at him.

She leaned into his caress. Butterflies filled her from the warmth of his smile. She was the one who was amazed to have him. From this moment on, she intended to only give him positive surprises.

Rain streaked against the dusty glass as the carriage

rattled ever closer to London. The fear that had knotted her stomach began to ease. She had misjudged him. At least in one area.

Anthony *didn't* see her as nothing more than a mirror of her mother. As far as he was concerned, her value did not come from the circumstances of her birth. But then, from where? No matter how well he treated her, she would never be a highborn society lady. He might be able to look past it, but other people would not. The truth was too big a chasm.

Now that she was Mrs. Fairfax, women unaware of her past spoke to her like an equal. An entire blissful week had passed without being insulted, rebuffed, or propositioned even once. She must remember that.

She leaned her head against his shoulder with a sleepy sigh. If only being accepted by others were as easy as being accepted by Anthony. That would definitely be a life she would love to get used to. Her eyes drifted shut as she let herself dream.

"Charlotte?" Sometime later, Anthony touched her shoulder. "This is the final posting house. We're in London. Once we eat, we'll head to my parents' townhouse. They'll have dined hours ago."

London. She lifted her head and winced at a crick in her stiff neck. She'd slept for longer than she had realized.

Dusk was falling. The rain had eased. They were stopped in front of a posting house. "You don't want to go straight to your family?"

"I want food," he replied, his expression shuttered. "My parents' pantry has something of a capricious nature. Come. Let's have a hot supper."

She took his hand and let him hand her out of the carriage. He turned back to fetch their luggage.

A cold wind swept through the street, taking rubbish—and Charlotte's loosened bonnet—with it.

Some yards up the street, an inebriated gentleman with a glass of some murky drink in his hand managed to swipe the bonnet up as it tumbled past. He swaggered unsteadily in her direction. "This yours, lassie?"

She snatched the now grimy bonnet from his hands. "Thank you."

He frowned and leaned forward to squint at her. "Don't I know you?"

Suddenly aware of the curl of her freshly washed hair and the setting sun illuminating her telltale face with rosy light, she hurriedly shoved the dirty bonnet back onto her head.

It was too late.

"You're the dead spit of Judith Devon." His cracked lips curved into a lascivious grin. "Had her a time or two myself. You must be her daughter. Bet you like a good shag just as much as your mama, eh?"

Before Charlotte could do more than freeze panic at having to face one of her mother's many clients, a fist shot out and slammed into the man's jaw, knocking him to the ground.

Anthony's voice was icy with fury. "No one speaks to my wife with disrespect."

"N-no, sir," the gentleman stammered, wiping blood from his split lip. "I didn't know she was yours."

"Now you do." Anthony wrapped his arm about Charlotte's trembling shoulders and led her toward the posting house. "We'll leave the rubbish in the street."

A thousand emotions assailed her whirling mind at once. Shame at even a drunkard being able to identify her for what she was. Humiliation that Anthony should witness it happening. Shock that, for the first time in her life, someone had come to her defense. Amazement and wonder at the realization that Anthony was her protector—in the true sense of the word. Not the demeaning one.

He didn't pay her for the use of her body. He respected her and required others to do the same. Her heart pounded.

She took a shaky breath and leaned closer to Anthony to catch her breath. Warmth began to ease back into her limbs. This wouldn't be the last time she was accosted on the street.

But this time, she wouldn't have to face it alone.

Chapter 17

By the time their hack rolled to a stop in front of his parents' townhouse, Anthony was a jumble of nervous anticipation. Not because he didn't know how his parents would react to his unexpected arrival. But because he knew all too well.

His parents' world revolved around money. When they had extra, they were buoyant and gay. But when they were in arrears… Anthony swallowed. He did his best to keep his family afloat.

From the moment he'd first sneaked into a gaming den at the age of fourteen, he had done his best to come home with his pockets heavy with gold. Despite his spendthrift proclivities, he was the closest to *reliable breadwinner* they'd ever had. His parents were too focused on blending with the ton.

This time, he had brought an even bigger surprise. Something far more lasting than a mere gaming purse. Today he would present them with a daughter-in-law.

Anthony's chest tightened. His mother would not be pleased at the prospect of one more mouth to feed. Providing for a wife would have an impact on his ability to provide for his parents.

His mother and father had to realize that, at some point, their son would take a wife… but they undoubtedly did not expect such a change to be imminent.

Neither had Anthony.

But although the timing was less than ideal and his pocketbook had never been poorer, Charlotte herself was worth more than gold.

He swung his wife out of the hack and on to the short pathway leading up to the front door. After flipping the jarvey an extra farthing to follow with the trunks, he took her hand and marched up to bang the brass knocker. His entire body was giddy with energy.

For a long moment, nothing happened.

He straightened his waistcoat. Nothing happened. He adjusted his cravat. Still no answer. Charlotte's blue eyes were fixed on the door, her cheeks pale with trepidation. He frowned and banged the knocker anew. His elation dimmed.

Even if his parents were not at home, certainly a servant would answer the door. Unless, of course, his parents had once again run out of coin to pay the staff. He rubbed his temples.

The difference between his parents with money and his parents without money… He checked his pocket watch. It was after ten. Perhaps he and Charlotte should reserve an inn for the night and call another day.

The door cracked open. Moonlight lit a sliver of

his mother's nervous countenance. She flung the door open wide.

He sketched a bow. "Good evening, Mother. Miss me?"

"Anthony," she squealed. She grabbed his lapels and kissed both his cheeks. "You are just in time."

"Supper?" he asked, incredulous. "At this late hour?"

"What? No. There was barely enough roast duck for your father and I to share. Not to mention that it was half burned." She fanned her throat. "You're just in time to pay the maid-of-all-work. Scroggs is the only one we have left. She cooks a terrible duck, but you know how doing work of any kind ruins my fingernails. She's in the kitchen now. I told her she wasn't to come out until she'd scrubbed every speck of black off those pots, and only then would we discuss her salary. Thank goodness you have arrived, so as not to make a liar of me!"

Poor Scroggs. Anthony's shoulders tensed under the weight of his responsibilities. His parents needed his ready money. They always did. But how could he rescue them when he couldn't even save himself?

"Can we discuss overdue wages once we've come inside, Mother?" He slid his arm around Charlotte's waist and pulled her closer. "I've someone I would like you to meet."

"Oh!" his mother gasped. "I am mortified. Discussing finances in front of an audience is unforgivably vulgar. Come in, child. Enter." She turned her head toward the kitchen. "Scroggs! We have guests!" She turned back to Anthony with hopeful eyes. "That maid is dreadfully overworked. Might we employ a butler?"

Embarrassed, he pulled Charlotte and their traveling trunks into the townhouse and shut the door firmly behind them. "Charlotte, this is my mother, Mrs. Margaret Fairfax. Mother, I'd like you to meet my wife, Mrs. Charlotte Fairfax."

"Your *what?*" his mother screeched in horror. "Anthony, how could you? You know how much I *love* a wedding. Your sister was such a disappointment in that regard, what with having a private ceremony in the Duke of Ravenwood's London estate and not even inviting us—I shall never forgive her—and you've gone and done the same. Can't you try to be thoughtful?"

"See?" he told Charlotte with a wry face. "To my mother, a private wedding being held at a ducal estate is far more scandalous than the reason for the secrecy. My sister was eight months pregnant at the time."

"Closer to nine, I should think," his mother mused as she led them toward the sitting room. "The twins came right after." She sent a horrified glance toward Charlotte's midsection. "She's not—You didn't—"

"No, no," he assured her. His sins were many, but they were always crimes against himself. His mother need not have worried. "Any grandchildren will arrive well after the requisite nine-month mark. Where's Father? I would like to present Charlotte to him, too."

"At his club, I'm afraid." His mother gave a long-suffering sigh. "I wish he wouldn't drink so. Anthony, if you could dash over tomorrow perhaps, and settle your father's account at White's, he would be ever so grateful. He has precious little credit left."

"Mother…" He eased onto the sofa and pulled

Charlotte down beside him. "Listen to me. I'm afraid I'm well into dun territory, myself, and have little coin to spare."

His mother perched on the edge of a chaise longue opposite them and waved his words away. "Who isn't stretched thin these days? You should see the lengthy accounts I accumulate just by keeping properly attired for the Season. I had to switch modistes to order new gowns just so I could start a new account! You cannot imagine the humiliation."

Guilt squeezed Anthony's chest. He leaned forward, his voice urgent. He had to make her understand. "Mother, please hear me. I'm all to pieces. Up the River Tick. Knocked into horse-nails. Empty pockets, Mother. I haven't a spare ha'penny. If I don't pay my creditors within a week, I'll spend the rest of my life in Marshalsea. The situation is deadly serious. Do you understand?"

She blinked, cast a sidelong glance at Charlotte, then fixed him with a wounded look. "If that excuse were remotely true, mightn't you think it an inopportune moment to take on the responsibility of a bride? Clearly it's not as awful as that. If you don't wish to help your parents, just say so. When the lease runs up, we'll go back to the country and… and *manage*. We always do."

Anthony's stomach clenched. How he wished her suspicions were true. He had never been able to turn his parents down when they needed a bit of blunt. But this time, he would have to. And his parents might have to "manage" on their own for far longer than they might think.

"Charlotte and I had a somewhat unplanned elopement," he explained, careful to avoid sharing too many details. "I found out how tenuous my situation was the following morning. You are correct. It was the most inopportune of moments. But right now, every penny I can find must go toward keeping me out of prison. Or at least reducing the length of my stay."

His mother paled. She turned her wide eyes not to him, but to Charlotte. "It's true? They can take Anthony away?"

"They *will* take him away," Charlotte corrected grimly as she slid her hand into his. "Unless we can raise enough money to stop it."

"I got myself into this scrape," he started to remind her.

Charlotte held up her other palm. "I'm your wife. Now it's *our* debt."

He tightened his jaw. That wasn't how it was supposed to work. *He* was the man. The provider. The law bestowed ownership of all property on the husband because the husband was meant to use his resources to protect the wife. Not leave her abandoned and penniless. Right along with his parents.

How on earth would he be able to take care of his family from prison? The reason his parents loved him so much was because he indulged them at every opportunity. Once he was gone, they would lose their home. They might even end up in debtors' prison alongside him.

"We can't let that happen." His mother wrung her thin hands, eyes wide with desperation. "We sold everything of value last year when we were evicted from the old townhouse. Your father hasn't a single book left in his library. The most expensive thing in this house is the one fine gown I intend to wear all Season. I commissioned a host of interchangeable trims so that no one will realize I'm always wearing the same dress. How can I help when we have no money to give you?"

Anthony blinked. He hadn't realized his mother had ever taken any cost-saving measures in her life, much less that she actively thought ahead to try and minimize debt. Her complaints about his father's visits to the club were now colored in a different light. Perhaps it was not the drinking she objected to after all, but rather the associated account they could never manage to settle. And the extra burden on her son.

"I shall have to sack Scroggs." She took a shaky breath. "The poor girl. And your father will simply have to do without the club. He cannot argue. 'Twas past time. How we shall entertain ourselves in an empty house with nary a book to read, I have no idea. I suppose I shall be too busy scrubbing pots to have time for frivolity anyway. The silver!" Her eyes suddenly lit up. "What if we sell the silver? And your grandmother's porcelain dining ware? How much do you owe the creditors? Will that do?"

Her questions robbed Anthony of the ability to speak. All the porcelain in Mayfair wouldn't repay his debt, but the important thing, the inconceivable thing, was that his mother would sacrifice it. His heart wrenched. That dining ware was by far her most valued possession. Something she protected so fiercely, no maid in London was allowed to touch it. She treated each piece like riches on display at a palace.

And she would sell it all without hesitation.

For Anthony.

"I have family jewelry of my own," Charlotte said. "Perhaps you'd care to accompany me on a visit to a pawnbroker? I cannot think of a worthier cause than Anthony."

"We'll all go," his mother said with determination. "His father might still have something valuable we could sell. There can be no greater emergency than this." She patted Anthony's arm despite the panic shimmering in her eyes. "Don't worry, son. Everything's going to be all right."

He swallowed the truth. Less than a week remained. But even if he couldn't save himself, he could not allow his fate to destroy his parents.

Charlotte squeezed his hand, her blue gaze intense. "I can tell by your face that you think our efforts will not be enough. Even if you're right, even if we sell the garments off our backs and they still take you away, *I will get you out.*"

Anthony's heart flipped and he pulled her close. She was more treasure than he deserved. He held her tight. Breathed in the scent of her hair.

She clutched him as if she would never let him go.

His throat stung. Although they hadn't exchanged traditional vows, she was on his side, for richer or for poorer. He glanced over at his mother. His parents were, too. They would all look out for each other.

This was what having family truly meant.

Chapter 18

When morning came, Charlotte awoke to find Anthony kneeling before his open trunk in search of some item within.

She rubbed her eyes. They hadn't unpacked their traveling bags the night before, in part because they had been too exhausted to do so… but primarily because the only furniture in the bedchamber was the bed.

At some point when times had been tough, Anthony's parents had sold the wardrobe, the dressing table, even the shaving mirror. Charlotte pushed herself up on her elbows and gazed about the empty chamber in renewed astonishment. A small pitcher of water was the sole nod to luxury.

She had been so *jealous* of these people. Not the Fairfaxes specifically, but people like them. People *less* than the Fairfaxes. Hadn't she dreamed of being a cobbler's daughter, a blacksmith's daughter, anything but what she was? If this was how poor fashionable people lived, what must home life have been like for the poor but respectable children who had spat at her in the streets?

Probably worse than her own. The revelation stunned her.

As a young girl, the weight of her mother prostituting herself had been all Charlotte could feel, all she could see. She'd been too hurt, too ashamed to consider that perhaps the reason her mother didn't quit her profession was because she didn't want Charlotte to grow up without food or clothing.

She couldn't imagine the childhood Anthony must have had. Rich one moment, in abject poverty the next. Selling clothes, books, anything. It was clear that his mother loved him. It was equally clear that no one in his family could be trusted with so much as a farthing. Not if they were still making the same mistakes. Living on credit and wishful thinking.

Little wonder Anthony had reached the predicament he was in. He was too fashionable to pursue a trade, too poor to resist the allure of making a fortune with a simple wager. Caught in the middle.

She took another look at the bare walls, the carpetless floor. Posting houses were more luxurious. Even if Anthony had wished to pursue a trade or business management, with what capital would he have made his investment? She ran her fingers over the threadbare blanket. All possible paths had led him straight to the gaming tables… and to ruin.

"You're awake." Anthony pushed up from the floor with a smile. "How did you sleep?"

"Very well, thank you," she lied. The tester and curtains were missing from the bed, and the draft from the window had given her gooseflesh every time the wind blew. She sat up. "I see you're already dressed. Are you parents early risers, too?"

"Not unless midday is early." His lips curved in self-deprecation. "I used to be even worse. All night in the vice parlors, all morning making up for lost sleep." His amusement faded. "I suppose I'll have plenty of time to sleep in Marshalsea."

"*No*," she said sharply. "The Duke of Courteland's will remains to be read. Perhaps my sire made me sole heiress of all his riches."

Anthony's face twisted, but he made no comment.

He didn't have to. Charlotte's shoulders slumped. They both knew how improbable that was. Any man who couldn't be bothered with her while he was alive could hardly be expected to care a whit once he was dead.

After she had washed and dressed, Charlotte upended the contents of their purses atop the bed. It had become something of an obsession to count their money every night. And every morning. But no matter how many times she sorted the bills and coins into small, short piles, they never added up to enough. What they needed was a miracle.

A knock sounded on the front door.

Anthony frowned. "It's far too early for a social call."

Her stomach dropped. "Maybe it's the debt collectors."

He headed to the door all the same. Scroggs would

not be doing the honors. The maid had been given her pay last night, along with several glowing letters of recommendation. She had made her escape posthaste. There was no one left to answer the door.

Charlotte started to follow, then hung back just out of sight. This was London. She could not let her comfort at being with Anthony make her forget the harsh reality of the world outside. The last thing she wished was to be treated with contempt right here in his parents' house.

But as mortifying as such an experience would be, it would be even more humiliating to know that she'd harmed his parents' reputation by her mere presence.

Anthony opened the creaky door. "Yes?"

"I'm terribly sorry to bother you," gushed a female voice, "but I am in a dreadful way. One of the ladies in my book club told me I simply must speak to Mrs. Fairfax, who will put everything to rights. Have I called at the correct address?"

"I'm afraid my mother is still abed. If you'd like to leave a calling card—"

"Your *mother?*" sputtered the female voice. "Oh, no. I'm looking for a *young* Mrs. Fairfax. Not a day over twenty, I'm told. Pretty face, yellow hair…"

Charlotte's heart thumped. The caller was looking for *her?*

She stepped around the corner before she could lose her courage. "Good morning. I'm Mrs. Fairfax. How may I help you?"

A completely unfamiliar matron wearing an exquisite fur-lined pelisse and a breathtaking diamond necklace stood in the doorway. To Charlotte's utter shock, not only did the woman's face light up upon spotting her, but the lady also bobbed slightly, as if giving a hurried curtsey.

Charlotte's mouth fell open in disbelief. She had never been curtsied to in all her life. Had never even dreamed of it.

And it had happened right here. In front of Anthony!

"It *is* you. I am certain of it." The lady clasped her silk-gloved hands together. "You absolutely must come with me at once. That is, at your earliest convenience. I shall pay extra. The situation, you see, is dire. I am having an absolute crisis with the downstairs maids, and my housekeeper has threatened to find other employment. I cannot possibly lose her! Mrs. Trimble has worked at Roundtree Manor longer than I've been alive."

Charlotte stared at her. A crisis with the downstairs maids? At Roundtree Manor?

"Lady Roundtree." Anthony sketched a quick bow. "Forgive me for not immediately recognizing you."

"Never mind niceties, young man. I am in positive jeopardy. A baronetcy may not compare to a duchy or an earldom, but it is my duty to see it run just as efficiently. Except the details have always been Mrs. Trimble's responsibility. Heavens, I've never even spoken to the servants. I would be lost! My dear, you are my last hope. Mrs. Podmore said you sorted out her governess issues in a trice. Do say you'll come to Roundtree Manor and sort out my housekeeper at once. You may name your price."

"Your predicament does sound appalling," Anthony said with a glance at his pocket watch. "Unfortunately, Mrs. Fairfax is booked solid the rest of the morning."

Charlotte slanted a shocked stare in his direction.

"But if you would like to send a coach for her at six o'clock this evening," he continued easily, "I am certain my wife can spare a moment to speak with your staff before they begin to prepare the evening meal. Provided you recompense her handsomely, of course."

"Yes," Lady Roundtree gushed. "This absolutely must be resolved before supper. It shall be as you say. A coach will be right on that corner, promptly at six. Thank you so very much."

When the door closed behind Lady Roundtree, Charlotte launched herself at Anthony. "That was the wealthy old biddy we needed. Why would you tell her I'm booked solid? What if she had shrugged and walked away?"

"For one," Anthony said as he swung her in celebratory circles, "proper ladies never *shrug*."

She pulled out of his embrace. "I'm serious. What if she had left? We *need* this money. *You* need this money."

"Not just this money—two thousand quid." Anthony took her hand. "Trust me, darling. I live in this world. Never let them believe getting what they want will be easy. By appearing selective and exclusive, your price undoubtedly just tripled." He grinned. "Whatever she offers to pay you, double it. And don't blink an eye."

"Double it?" Charlotte choked. She had no idea

how much Lady Roundtree believed speaking to a housekeeper was worth, but the sum was no doubt far more exorbitant than the task merited. "Why would she pay it?"

He clasped his hands together and affected a pose of sweeping tragedy. "Because it is a *crisis*, darling. The lady is in *positive jeopardy*."

Charlotte burst out laughing at his dramatic rendition. But more than humor, he had given her a measure of hope. If Anthony could not amass enough money to stay out of prison, she would offer every penny she owned to buy them even a few more weeks together.

He stroked the back of her hand. "Now that you have a day of freedom, how would you like to spend it?"

There was only one answer. She bit her lip. "If you would grant me permission, I am desperate to see my mother. She is the only thing I ever loved in this city—the only one who ever loved me—and I have missed her dreadfully these past few weeks."

"Permission?" he repeated in surprise. "You don't need my permission to see your family. I'd like *your* permission to accompany you. If you'll have me, of course."

At first, she couldn't make sense of his words. Surely she had mistaken his meaning. "Accompany me?"

"Your mother," he repeated, his gaze earnest. "I'd like to meet her."

Charlotte's heart beat faster. Did he understand what he was asking? What it would mean for him to pay a social call on a courtesan? What it would mean to Charlotte for someone to treat her mother like a woman worthy of respect? How it would kill her if, despite his best efforts, high society distaste still shone through?

"I don't know," she stammered. What would he think of her mother? What would her mother think of him? She didn't want either to be hurt. She had done enough of that herself. The last time she'd spoken to her mother, they hadn't parted company on the best of terms. "I swore I wouldn't go back until I had changed my fortune. Until I could provide for her for a change. Until I could prove I was *worth* something."

Anthony tilted his head in surprise. "You are worth everything." He lifted her fingers to his lips. "I may not be as eloquent as Lady Roundtree, but I value you very, very much. That's why I'd like to meet your mother. So I can get to know you even better. And the woman who made you."

She gazed up at him doubtfully, then swallowed her objections. Before she could change her mind, she gave a short nod in acquiescence.

A smile bloomed over his face.

She gathered her courage and smiled back. Now that the plan was made, she couldn't wait to be on her way.

"Do you mind if we leave posthaste?" She glanced over her shoulder at the silent, empty townhouse. There was certainly nothing requiring their immediate attention here. Not until Lady Roundtree came back. "We should take care to return by six. I seem to recall some sort of critical appointment on my agenda."

"Life and death," he agreed. "I promise you'll be

home in time to fleece that goosecap out of scads of money."

Home. Pleasure spread through her at his choice of words. Not because she aspired to share a townhouse with his parents. But because he was right. Any place they were together felt like home.

But what would he think of her childhood home? The area she'd grown up in? Would he judge her or her mother for the activities that took place beneath that roof in order to keep them both clothed and fed?

She pushed her misgivings aside as he hailed a hackney cab. She continued to keep a brave face as she gave the direction to the jarvey, who raised his eyebrows at the address. Her neck heated. Either the driver recognized the neighborhood… or he'd made plenty of stops at Charlotte's house.

She did her best to remain placid as the hack pulled to a stop before her mother's townhouse.

"This the place?" the jarvey asked, giving them a speculative look.

In silence, Charlotte gave him an extra coin.

She stood on the edge of the cobbled road next to Anthony as the hack rolled away. The street looked the same. The houses. The people. Just coming this far made her feel as though she was slipping back into her old self. To the defiant little girl who loved her mother dearly but publicly denied any relation to the whore on the corner. To the despairing young woman who fled in search of a father who had never existed. To escape a world that had only brought shame. To bring home a better life.

Apprehension made the air feel like molasses. She

took Anthony's hand and led him up the walk to the front door. She wasn't certain if she gripped his fingers for strength—or to keep him from running away when he realized what he had done.

This was her reality. She couldn't rewrite the past. For better or for worse, this was where she had come from. Where part of her would always be.

The door swung open before her knuckles had even touched the knocker. Her mother stood before her wearing an expression of shock and pleasure.

Hesitant, Charlotte gazed back at her mother's familiar countenance. With so few years between them, was it any wonder they were mirror images?

One had to look closely to find the differences in her mother's face. Tiny lines crinkled at the edges of identical blue eyes. A few strands of gray blended with identical golden curls. They shared the same height, the same curves, the same smile.

Except neither of them was smiling now. Her mother's surprised eyes were glassy with unshed tears.

"I thought you weren't coming back," she gasped. "I thought you were never coming back."

"You knew it was a fool's mission. I thought I knew better," Charlotte admitted with self-deprecation. "May I come in?"

Her mother pulled her forward and into her arms. "You can. Of course you can. You can stay as long as you like. This will always be your home."

Mixed emotions assailed Charlotte as she returned her mother's embrace. She didn't want this to be her home. She abhorred every memory she held of this place.

And yet it contained her mother. Someone who Charlotte had never stopped loving. Who would always be an important part of her family.

She leaned back to pull Anthony across the threshold. "This is Mr. Anthony Fairfax."

Her mother shot her a startled look out of the corner of her eye.

"No," Charlotte choked out in embarrassment. "He's not here for that. Anthony is my husband. Darling, this is my mother. Miss Judith Devon."

He sketched a grandiose bow. "The pleasure is indeed mine."

Her mother stared in disbelief, then dipped an equally elegant curtsey.

"The pleasure…" Scarlet flooded her cheeks as she turned toward Charlotte. "A *husband*. Does he—did you—"

"Yes. He knows." Charlotte led them into the front salon, which was just as elegant as it always was, if a little worn at the edges. "That is partly why I'm here."

Her mother frowned. "What do you mean?"

Charlotte pulled a ruby earring from her reticule. "Who gave these to you?"

Her mother's eyes lowered. "That affair was so long ago. It doesn't matter anymore. It never mattered."

"It mattered to me," Charlotte said softly. "It mattered to a little girl who longed for a father."

Her mother's shoulders crumpled. "I never meant for you to be born ruined. I wanted to be a good mother to my baby, but my only choices were to keep you or leave you on the steps of a church. And I couldn't leave you. I loved you before you took your first breath."

Charlotte's throat tightened. As a small child, she had often fantasized about running away to an orphanage so that some other family could adopt her. A family respectable enough that, someday, Charlotte could marry well and come back to rescue her mother. So that they could both have a happy ending.

Her mother met her gaze. "You may think I made the wrong decision, and that's your right. But being sold to a workhouse isn't better than the life you had. I grew up in a workhouse. Many children don't live long enough to leave. Some, like me, leave the only way they can." Her eyes were haunted. "I didn't want that for my daughter. I didn't want you dead, and I didn't want you wishing you *were* dead while you were on your back in some alley. So I did the best I could."

"I don't blame you for being a courtesan," Charlotte admitted in a rush. "I always knew you were trying to give me the best life you could. But the harder you worked to raise money, the more infamous and disrespectable we became."

"That wasn't the plan." Her mother's sad smile didn't meet her eyes. "I thought the life of a kept woman would turn out differently. I was quite sought after, once. For one whirlwind year, I wasn't a mere strumpet, but a fashionable courtesan. I thought I had it all. Operas, fireworks, romance. I was toasted at every turn. It still seems like a dream."

"What happened?" Anthony asked, his voice gentle.

"I got pregnant," she replied bluntly. "No one wants a mistress who cannot control her own body." Her chin lifted. "And then I committed the second worst sin. I kept my baby." She cast Charlotte a rueful look. "Once I was no longer a desirable catch, I had to be much less choosy about who I accepted as clients."

Charlotte swallowed. Of course, the "protectors" had become far less protective. Guilt snaked through her. A woman in her mother's shoes was not elegant, but desperate.

Her mother's gaze unfocused. "I didn't want a four-year-old knowing words like 'courtesan' or 'protector,' so I spoke in code as best I could. Instead of sexual favors, I offered bedtime stories. Instead of paying clients, a *dìonadair* would visit."

"*Dìonadair*," Charlotte whispered. "I thought it was his name."

Her mother laughed without humor. "It was everyone's name. I picked each man's best characteristics, and those were the stories I told you. One day, Dìonadair would be a gallant rake, who always invited the wallflowers to dance. Another day, Dìonadair would be a great scholar, with the finest scientific mind in all of England."

"I meant… I meant my father," Charlotte explained through her scratchy throat. "I thought the Duke of Courteland's name was Dìonadair."

"The Duke of—how do you know that?" Her mother shot up straight, eyes wild. "Who told you?"

"Not him." Charlotte's voice grew thick. "He's dead."

"Oh, love." Her mother fell to her knees before

Charlotte and took her hands. "You were so *angry* with me for not giving you a father. You thought I didn't know who it was. But I always knew. It was better that you never met. He wouldn't have been what you wanted."

Not want a duke? Charlotte's mouth flattened. She and her father should have been given the choice to decide that for themselves. But they'd never had a chance.

Her mother gazed up at her, eyes pleading. "I grew up without love. Without a mother or a father. When I left the workhouse, no one cared. No one missed me. I didn't want that for you." She gripped Charlotte's hands. "I didn't want to give you a father who didn't care. I wanted to give you a mother who *did.* I never wanted you to doubt for a single moment that the one parent you do have loves you with all her soul."

Charlotte's anger began to dissipate. Would she really have been better off knowing who her father was, but that he didn't care to meet her? Her shoulders slumped. She supposed sometimes there were no good choices.

Her mother sighed. "I would do anything for you, love. I *have* done. More than I care for you to know. When you left, I felt as if the sun had been ripped from the sky. I didn't just miss you—I mourned. I knew you were never coming back. Who would want a whore for a mother?" Her mouth twisted in self-recrimination. "All I wanted to be was a good parent. All I ever was, was a disappointment. To us both." Her eyes shimmered. "No matter how hard I tried, no matter how much I loved you, I failed you from the moment of your birth."

Charlotte's throat grew thick. Her mother's only wish had been for her daughter to love her. To accept her. Her stomach twisted. The very things she herself had longed to receive, she had withheld from her own mother. Shame filled her for her years of blindness.

She slid off the couch and into her mother's arms.

"I do love you," she confessed as she buried her face in her mother's hair and held on for dear life. "I always have. You're the reason I wanted to find us a better life."

Chapter 19

It was four o'clock in the afternoon by the time Anthony realized he had spent all day with a courtesan, doing things no man of his acquaintance had ever done before: discussing the impact of Miss Devon's profession on her life and her child, and complimenting her on what a splendid individual her daughter had grown up to be.

Charlotte glanced his way as he returned his pocket watch to his waistcoat. "Is it time?"

He hated to break up their reunion. Lady Roundtree could wait—he hoped. "Only if you'd still like to make the other appointment."

His wife hesitated, then nodded. "We desperately need the money. I cannot let my name become synonymous with someone who doesn't keep her word. Although I suppose that's an improvement over—" She winced and color bloomed in her cheeks. "I'm sorry, Mother. I didn't mean…"

Miss Devon shook her head, her tone rueful. "We have both said plenty we didn't mean. I do understand."

"There's a lady who wishes me to intervene in some row between her servants. As preposterous as it sounds, she's willing to pay me for my insight into the minds of the lower classes." Charlotte pushed to her feet. "Who knew humble origins would one day be considered 'expert knowledge'?"

Miss Devon rose to walk them to the door. "Will you come back soon?"

"Very soon," Charlotte promised, her smile shy.

Anthony kissed his mother-in-law's hand, then led his wife to the street. The coal-tinged wind chilled his face and fingers. Hailing a hack was taking much longer than he had anticipated.

After glimpsing him check his pocket watch for what must have been the tenth time, Charlotte lifted a wry shoulder. "Fares are less plentiful, and less desirable, this far from Mayfair."

He stared at her, startled to realize how dramatically one's address changed one's perception of how the world worked. He gazed at the endless row of houses just like Charlotte's. How many of their inhabitants were long used to waiting for hackney cabs that never came? He swallowed. The lower classes had far fewer opportunities in countless ways… regardless of the size of their pocketbooks.

Once they were finally inside a hack, he put his arm around his wife and held her close.

She snuggled into his side. "When I return from Lady Roundtree's, I'll give you my jewelry. If there's no inheritance money, you'll be able to bargain a better price with a pawnbroker than I would."

He shook his head. "I can't sell them. Your rubies remind you of your father."

"Not anymore." Her mouth tightened. "Now they symbolize my mother, and her innumerable sacrifices for me."

He frowned. "Then why would you want to give them away?"

"Because she's not the only one who can make a sacrifice for someone she cares about." Charlotte's eyes didn't leave his. "Promise me you'll pawn them. It's for us."

Warmth filled his heart as he gazed down at her upturned face. Handing over her most valuable possession wasn't just a sacrifice. It was trust. She was placing her faith in him not to take the money and gamble it away. She believed he was worth the risk.

He set his jaw with determination. Charlotte was also worth sacrifice. If there was any way to stay out of prison without selling her sole heirloom, he was determined to find it.

"I promise we'll sell your jewels only as a last resort," he said at last. He would strip nothing from her if it could be helped. "Those rubies mean too much to you for me to pawn them without knowing if I'll be able to earn them back someday."

Her solemn blue eyes stared up at him for a long moment before she returned her head to its resting place against his shoulder.

He pressed a kiss to her hairline, in awe that, of all

the women who he might have found himself accidentally betrothed to, *this* was the one he'd been fortunate enough to capture.

What she perceived as her greatest flaw—being born the child of a courtesan—didn't bear the least reflection on her own character. He didn't care a fig about her past, or the reputation of her family members. The last thing he wanted was for her to feel that she needed to be someone she was not. Her mother was a delight, and loved Charlotte exactly as she was. So did Anthony.

He froze in realization. Good Lord. *He loved her.*

A rueful laugh rumbled within him at the thought. He'd beaten the dealer. Now he just had to deserve the trust she'd placed in him. He leaned his cheek against the top of her head.

When the hack turned onto his parents' road, Lady Roundtree's extravagant coach-and-four was already waiting for Charlotte at the corner. Anthony instructed the jarvey to pull alongside.

"You'll do splendidly," he assured his wife as he handed her from one carriage to the other. "All that's required is your mind."

"I'll try not to lose it on the way to Roundtree Manor," she said wryly.

Anthony grinned. He doubted the baroness had enough brains to note the difference. "Just remember—no matter what price she offers, ask for double."

After the coach-and-four drove away, the hack's jarvey looked down from his perch "Be needing my services for anything else?"

Anthony reached into his pocket for a coin. "No,

I—"

"*There* you are!" came a rough voice from behind Anthony's shoulder. "We been standing at your door for an hour."

Full of dread, he turned to see the two ruffians who had confronted him at the Kitty and Cock Inn. He tipped his hat to belie his nerves. "Good afternoon, gentlemen. How may I be of service?"

"You can give Gideon back his blunt."

"I am making great strides toward that task." Anthony hoped his cheerful smile masked the lie. "Didn't you gentlemen say I was entitled to a fortnight's grace period?"

"*Was*." The first ruffian bared his jagged teeth. "Better hurry. You've only a few days left to make good."

"This oughta help motivate you." The pockmarked ruffian shoved a folded document at Anthony's chest.

He smoothed open the parchment as if it contained nothing more urgent than a request from his grandmother to visit her for tea.

It did not.

Fear gripped him when he saw the stamp on the bottom of the parchment. The document was a summons to surrender his money or his person four days hence. His stomach dropped. This was it. There was no way out.

"Superb," he assured the enforcers. "Who doesn't love an invitation? I shall be certain to note the date in my schedule."

"See that you do." Pockmark's eyes were cold.

Broken Tooth smirked. "You don't want us to have to escort you there."

An understatement. Anthony hoped his hands didn't shake as he folded the parchment and shoved it into his greatcoat. Devil take it! He had to think of something.

Once the ruffians departed, the jarvey glanced down at Anthony with a far less congenial expression. "Got that farthing you owe me, mate?"

"Two of them." He tossed up the coins and leaped back inside the cab before the hack could leave. "Drive me to the Cloven Hoof, please."

The jarvey sent him a doubtful glance. "The gaming hell?"

Anthony grimly gazed out the window. "The very one."

It might be his only shot.

Not for gambling. Especially not with his wife's rubies. Anthony would have to keep himself away from the tables, come what may. He was going to the Cloven Hoof to plead for mercy from its owner. He could pay every penny if he had more time. Surely the lord of a vice parlor had plenty of gold. What would a few months' reprieve hurt before collecting on Anthony's debts?

Presuming the man could be made to see reason.

He and Maxwell Gideon had once been friends. In fact, when Anthony had first discovered Gideon had become the owner of Anthony's IOUs to save him from other gamblers' wrath, he'd believed the man had done him a great favor. Certainly a friend would be more understanding of the vagaries of good fortune.

Particularly a man who ran a vice parlor of his own.

But Anthony had been wrong. About everything.

Not just wrong… He had been foolhardy. Immature. Careless. But he wasn't that man anymore. He was happy to take responsibility. Proud to, in fact.

He just needed more than four short days to do so.

The hack dropped him off at the Cloven Hoof's main entrance. The nondescript building didn't look like much from the outside, with its dark windows and scuffed brick walls. But it was the one gaming establishment in London that still opened its doors to Anthony Fairfax.

He hoped.

Head held high and an easy smile plastered on his face, he strode up to the door and gave the coded knock.

To his immense relief, he recognized the enforcer who cracked open the door. "Vigo."

The burly enforcer inclined his head. "Fairfax."

"I've come to see Gideon."

"Got an appointment?"

"Ask him."

Vigo shut the door without further comment.

His nerves sizzling with unease, Anthony laced his hands behind his neck to wait.

This would work. Six o'clock in the evening was far too early for the Cloven Hoof to be crowded. Gideon *had* to see him.

Whether Anthony could convince him to call off his hounds was another matter entirely.

The door swung open and Vigo motioned him inside. "He's in the back."

With a smile far more carefree than Anthony's churning gut would indicate, he crossed the threshold into the gaming hell.

Low-hung chandeliers illuminated rows of worn tables surrounded by clumps of bright-eyed gentlemen. Dice clattered across hazard tables, followed by the whoops or cries of the spectators. Cards flew across felt green Faro tables before the banker gathered the chips. In every corner was a different game. A different opportunity to win big—or to lose it all.

Anthony's blood sang from his proximity to so many gaming tables.

"Fairfax," Lord Wainwright called out. "Knew you'd be back. Care to roll the dice with me?"

Anthony's heart raced at the thought. Every particle of his body longed to do just that. Roll the dice. Play the cards. Make the wagers. But those days were done.

"Some other time," he called back. "I'm just here to see Gideon."

"Fairfax not gamble?" came a disbelieving cackle from behind a *vingt-et-un* table. "The end times are upon us."

Anthony sent a quelling scowl in the direction of the voice, until he realized the speaker was Phineas Mapleton, an insufferable gossip not even worth the effort required to frown at him.

"If you're not going to wager," came a low voice in the opposite direction, "perhaps you'll have a drink with us."

Anthony turned to see the Duke of Lambley sharing a table with the penniless marquess Lord Hawkridge. Anthony's eyes widened in surprise. He had never pictured those two as friends. Then again, he supposed one never knew who the other guests were at Lambley's infamous masquerade parties.

"I'll stop by once I've spoken to Gideon," he promised, "but I can't stay long. I've a wife to get home to now."

"A *what?*" Whistles and good-natured ribbing filled the air. "What kind of woman would leg-shackle herself to you, Fairfax? You win her at the tables?"

"As it happens, the lady won me," he hedged, correctly anticipating the wild laughter and thumps on his shoulder. He raised his voice. "Besides being able to sweep the floor with any of you pups, Mrs. Fairfax has made quite a name for herself in the arena of advice-giving. If you've a sibling, wife, or parent in need of a good dose of common sense, my wife's ability to convince featherbrains to make logical choices is second to none."

"Explains you not gambling, I'd wager." Mapleton smirked. "Lord knows you aren't smart enough to walk away on your own."

Anthony smiled back. "And here you stand, holding dice in your palm, further making your point."

"Is she the one who helped Leticia Podmore hire her new governess?" Lord Hawkridge asked.

"The very one." Anthony frowned in surprise. "How did you hear of that?"

The marquess pulled a face. "My aunt shares her book club. Apparently Mrs. Podmore was too busy boasting about her new governess to pay much attention to dissecting Radcliffe's latest gothic novel."

"Then you understand the level of skill and patience required of Mrs. Fairfax," Anthony replied with a grin. "If you'll excuse me, I've an appointment to keep."

Before anyone else could waylay him with talk of women or wagers, he strode to the rear office and stepped inside.

Gideon sat behind a large mahogany desk, reviewing a stack of paper. Inky black hair fell into equally dark eyes. An unfashionable hint of whiskers shadowed the line of his jaw.

He was at the gaming hell at least twelve hours a day, overseeing everything from each ha'penny in the till to the upkeep on the worn green baize of the Faro tables.

Anthony took a seat opposite the desk and removed his damp hat. "Your ruffians came to call."

Maxwell Gideon glanced up. "The lads mentioned they bumped into you in Scotland."

"And outside my parents' home, just a few moments ago."

"Clever." Gideon leaned back in his chair. "I'll have to increase their salaries."

"Why are you doing this?" Anthony clenched the ridge of his hat. "I could have sworn we were friends."

"I'd like to think we still are." Gideon gazed back at him blandly. "However, I didn't create your debts. *You* did. Their uncertain nature was causing mistrust and discontent in my gaming hell. I solved the problem. Now you owe the debt to me."

"I'm working on it." Anthony tried to keep the desperation from his tone and manner. "I've managed to earn a solid percentage of what I owe, and could gather enough to repay at least a quarter of the balance by tomorrow. But it will take months to save this kind of blunt. Not four days."

"You're *earning* funds," Gideon repeated with obvious interest. "And saving. How unlike you."

"Twenty-five percent," Anthony said. "I can give you twenty-five percent tomorrow, and another twenty-five percent… a month from now."

Gideon nodded slowly. "What date was listed on the document my employees delivered?"

Anthony pulled the folded parchment from his greatcoat pocket with trembling fingers. "Monday."

"Then I'll see you on Monday." Gideon returned his attention to the stacks of paper on his desk. "Bring one hundred percent."

Chapter 20

Anthony stormed out of Gideon's office and back into the gaming area. Instead of seeming as nostalgic and cheerful as they had moments ago, the candlelit card tables softened by cigar smoke and desperation were now darkly inviting.

Anger at Gideon had every nerve in Anthony's body on edge. His predicament was more than frustrating. It was impossible. He could never earn back the money in time doing anything respectable.

He glanced around the Cloven Hoof. But in a place like this, if he could just win one good wager…

"Fairfax," rumbled a voice from the corner. "Still have time for that drink?"

"Lambley." Anthony blinked. He had forgotten about the duke. The allure of the gambling tables had that effect on him. He rubbed his face. "I have never been in more dire need of strong spirits and good company. But not here. I can't… I have to get out."

"Very well." The duke rose to his feet. "I possess far better in my own cellar. Come." Lambley strode toward the exit. "My coach is always at the ready."

Anthony followed the duke outside.

Upon sight of the duke, a street urchin immediately ran off. Anthony turned to Lambley in surprise. "Was that boy's reaction to your presence or mine?"

"I paid him to react swiftly. My coach will arrive at any moment."

Before he had even finished his explanation, a stately black coach bearing the duke's crest glided around the corner, pulled by a gorgeous set of matching grays. The postilion leaped down to open the door.

Anthony entered after Lambley and arranged himself facing the rear.

"Shall we wait until we have wine in our goblets?" the duke asked. "Or would you like to tell me what the deuce could have you in such a state?"

Wine. Lots and lots of wine.

"I owe Gideon money," Anthony said dully.

Lambley's gaze pierced him. "When haven't you?"

"Wagonloads of money. More than I can pay."

"I see." Lambley leaned back. "What do you hope to gain from me? A loan?"

Anthony rested his head against the back of the carriage wall and covered his face with his hands. Was this his best attempt at responsibility? Robbing Peter to pay Paul in an endless series of loans until not a single friend remained?

With four days to spare, it was perhaps the only option he had left.

"I would need a way to pay you back," he admitted. "I don't have one. If you loan me money, I may only be delaying the inevitable."

Lambley gave Anthony a considering stare. "Hmm."

"Unless it wasn't a loan, precisely. What if it were an advance against wages earned?" Anthony gave a crooked smile. "I don't suppose your estate is in want of a new gardener?"

"Have you any skill at gardening?"

"I can't tell a daisy from a dandelion," Anthony admitted. "Besides gambling, I've no skills useful to our set at all. That's the crux of the problem."

The duke's gaze was impassive. "Businessmen generally invest in individuals with either talent or knowledge. Perhaps you have expertise in something I might find useful?"

If only he did! Anthony kneaded his temples and tried to think.

"I can't say that I have great knowledge in any field not taught to all gentlemen who attended Eton." He had paid for every penny of that hard-won education with windfalls at the gaming tables. "I speak the same amount of French, recall the same amount of history. The primary difference between myself and the average buck is that I'm fashionable enough to be a common guest amongst the *beau monde*, yet unfashionable enough to be just as recognizable amongst the fast set, and worse. There isn't a gaming hell in London unacquainted with my name."

"I see." Lambley steepled his fingers. "How familiar are you with Vigo's work?"

"With—" Anthony stared at him, thrown off guard by the abrupt change in subject. "What *is* Vigo's work? He guards the threshold to the Cloven Hoof, granting entrance to those with the proper background or qualifications, and turns away anyone who oughtn't to be let inside. Isn't that it?"

The duke raised his brows. "It seems like important work to me."

"Well… yes, I suppose so." Anthony smiled in self-deprecation. "Gideon can't have riffraff like myself inciting discontent amongst his clients by promising debts that cannot be paid."

"That is one type of inappropriate guest," Lambley agreed. "I should imagine there are many more. Vigo keeps out the street urchins, the penny harlots, the drunkards, any wayward fashionable ladies, the Prince Regent… It's the Lord's work, really."

Anthony chuckled hollowly. "Are you suggesting I ask Gideon for employment? He's made his position quite clear. I pay him, not the other way about."

The carriage stopped in front of the ducal residence.

Lambley stepped down from the coach and strode up to the entrance.

Anthony followed him inside and into a sumptuous parlor, stocked with a dozen comfortable chairs and at least as many glass decanters.

The duke poured them each a glass, then took a seat. "At last. Now we can discuss business. What do you recall about my masquerade parties?"

Anthony leaned back at the unexpected topic. The duke's scandalous masked balls were desirable for their exclusivity and legendary because of their secret rooms for sensual pleasures. Lambley got away with such chicanery because he was a duke—and a handsome, wealthy bachelor.

No member of the ton with any hope of preserving their reputation could ever admit to being anywhere near such a fête. Yet when Anthony had attended one the previous year, such a thick crush of masked partiers had filled the rooms that dancing was all but impossible.

"I don't think I'm overstating if I suggest your masquerades are scandalous," Anthony said dryly. "Everyone in attendance risks far more than their Almack's voucher just by walking through the door."

Lambley's eyes glinted. "You're assuming my guests were ever eligible for Almack's vouchers… or have a reputation to defend."

Anthony burst out laughing. "You're right. Having been to one of your masquerades, I can attest to having absolutely no idea who else was there. That's the irresistible part: having the anonymity to do anything one desires. Nobody will ever know. The guests themselves don't even know."

"But *I* know." Lambley's tone was mild, but his eyes were serious. "Nothing is ever completely anonymous. Admission is by invitation only, because I must keep out anyone likely to disturb other guests' comfort, either during the event or after. It also serves as insurance, should one guest complain about the behavior of another. Partygoers might see each other as Mr. Red Mask and Miss Blue Mask, but I must know their proper names in order to deal with each situation appropriately."

Anthony frowned. That much responsibility did indeed sound more like the security measures of a gaming hell than the fun-filled soirées of a careless rake, as Anthony had always imagined. Then again, he supposed that a masked ball of that caliber could be seen as the very definition of a den of iniquity. A vice parlor in society clothes. Accepting the invitation was a shockingly high wager indeed.

"How do you do it?" he asked. "How do you keep track of so many people?"

"I can't." Lambley sipped his port. "When I held my first masked gathering, I invited perhaps two dozen friends. It was diverting and easy. As my notoriety grew, so did the demand for invitations. My presence is needed amongst my guests, but I cannot mingle in the primary salons and guard the front door at the same time. My butler shoulders that task."

Anthony thought back. The masquerade inside had been so much more interesting than the mundane act of surrendering his umbrella and greatcoat that he hadn't given the process another thought. But now that he did… "I seem to recall him allowing entry to one person at a time. He took my invitation and jotted something down in a little book."

Lambley inclined his head. "The registry of invited guests contains the date, name, and identifying mask features of every person who attends the ball. To date, there have been no grave issues, but in the event something untoward should occur, it is vital to have the ability to ensure there are consequences."

Anthony nodded slowly. "That makes sense."

"Using my butler as an enforcer may sound logical. He is a trusted member of my staff, and answering doors is one of his primary duties. However, it offers him very little opportunity for rest. He must be at his post by daybreak for his regular duties, yet masquerade nights also tend to last until daybreak."

Anthony frowned. Working more than twenty-four hours in a row was an unhappy circumstance in any profession. Yet hiring a new staff member would mean entrusting the identities of guests who were jealously guarding their anonymity to an untested servant without the butler's years of experience and trust.

Hope prickled his skin. "Am I to understand that you are offering me employment?"

"The 'common knowledge' you dismiss so easily is the only reason I am considering it," Lambley said blandly. "I *have* had instances of stolen or forged invitations. If Lady X tells my butler that she is Mrs. Y, he will simply note it in the journal and allow her entry. You, however, would not be so easy to fool. With your background, you are likely to have made the acquaintance of both Lady X *and* Mrs. Y, and would be able to put paid to that nonsense at the door."

The duke was right. Anthony's hopes rose. Under the right circumstances, his social position bridging two worlds became an advantage, not a disadvantage.

"Furthermore," Lambley continued, "I have known you for two decades. You can't be trusted with a loose shilling, but you're a good man. You would never betray a confidence. The entire ton fully trusts in your character. When Lady X sees it is you at the door, she will not feel any less comfortable sharing her name than she does relinquishing it to my butler."

"There must be a catch." Anthony straightened. "It sounds as though I would be perfect for the role."

"You are. The role, however, may not be perfect for you. Not only would you bear responsibility for tracking every single identity without ever breathing a hint of the intelligence you gather. The guests themselves will also be aware of your identity. It shall not require but a moment for all of London to know that Mr. Anthony Fairfax is now the paid night butler at the Duke of Lambley's masked balls."

Anthony's stomach dipped. Accepting this lifeline would mean severing ties with a world he loved. The only life he'd ever known. The sort of future he'd imagined himself living. By accepting such scandalous employment, his societal standing would be ruined.

And as his wife, Charlotte would suffer the same fate.

Lambley didn't change expression. "Being in my employ is more than merely scandalous. If you take this position, you will no longer bridge both worlds. Your reputation amongst the smart set will be irrevocably destroyed."

The duke's warning seeped into Anthony's bones. Every word Lambley spoke was true. And yet, exchanging his status for his freedom wasn't just the best choice—it was Anthony's *only* choice. His sole chance to save himself, his marriage, and his future.

"A mask," he said suddenly. "I require leave to wear a mask."

Lambley arched a brow. "You require it, do you?"

Anthony gazed back impassively. "A mask won't affect my ability to do my job, but hiding my identity would help me protect my wife's reputation."

"You can wear a mask, but you can't hide your voice or your mannerisms. Some percentage of guests are still likely to recognize you."

"They can suspect all they like. They won't be able to prove it—or even to say how they know. Not without implicating themselves as attendees of such a scandalous event themselves."

"It is scandalous," Lambley reminded him. "Even with a mask. Are you certain this is the path you wish to take?"

The gossip would be nothing more than idle rumor.

Rumor that could ruin him… or clear his debts. And give him and Charlotte a chance at a real marriage. A new life. Free of fear from debtors' prison.

Anthony squared his shoulders. He didn't care about the smart set anymore. About being invited to dinner parties or being welcome at Almack's. He cared about setting things right. He cared about Charlotte. This was his sole chance to provide for her. To be there for her. Only a fool would say no.

"I'll do it," he said without hesitation.

"Then I shall have a contract drawn up at once." Lambley's eyes glittered in the candlelight. "I will settle your account with Gideon only after you've completed your first night to my satisfaction. At that point, you will be safe from prosecution or further retaliation from Gideon's enforcers. However, if at any time you default or fail to meet your obligations to me as specified in our contract…" The duke's tone was harsh and final. "You will not recover from the consequences."

Anthony nodded. He couldn't think about consequences. Failure was not an option. But even this opportunity—his only opportunity—might not save him. Not if his debts wouldn't be addressed until he completed his first night. He tried to swallow his panic. "When is your next ball?"

"Saturday."

His shoulders tensed. There might still be time. "I must repay Gideon by Monday or it will be too late."

"How much do you owe?" The duke gestured at a quill and ink on the sideboard. "Write it for me so I can pay the precise amount."

Cheeks flushing, Anthony forced himself to write *two thousand and forty pounds, thirteen shillings and sixpence* and handed Lambley the damning paper. There in black and white, the sum seemed astronomical… and he felt incredibly foolish.

"I see." Lambley returned the paper to the table. "Let's talk terms, shall we? Given the highly sensitive nature of the information you must protect, I will pay you quite handsomely. But until you have paid off your debt, all monies earned shall be placed against the principal. Two thousand pounds is not a sum I invest lightly. It may take a full year until you repay your debt or receive a single penny to take home. Are you amenable to these stipulations?"

Amenable? Anthony nearly melted in gratitude. The terms were leagues better than a lifetime in prison. Earning that much money in a single year was more than anyone of his stature could have dreamed. Paying off his debt before he took home a penny was only fair.

But the *following* year! Once he did take home his salary, he could finally treat Charlotte to the life she deserved. Hope filled him. This time next year, they could be safe.

Until then, he would concentrate on fulfilling his contract with the duke. If the loss of Anthony's reputation meant the loss of his friends, so be it. He would have an opportunity to stay with Charlotte, and she was all that mattered.

But it wasn't going to be easy. In order to keep her and his freedom, he would have to vanquish his reckless impulse to gamble for an entire year. Dance to Lambley's tune. The smallest slipup would ruin everything. Anthony could not let that happen.

He had already ruined enough.

The woman he loved had spent her entire life fighting to be considered respectable. She would be well within her rights to annul marriage to a man who harmed her reputation—and ruined her chance for a better future. His skin went cold.

What if his only chance to stay out of prison caused him to lose Charlotte anyway?

He curled his clammy fingers into fists. He could no longer imagine a life without Charlotte. Yet if she preferred an annulment to a life of ignominy, he would have no choice but to give it to her.

Until he knew for certain that Lambley would call off Gideon's debt collectors, Anthony could not raise Charlotte's hopes. He did not want to disappoint her yet again. Or make promises he couldn't keep.

His new arrangement would have to remain a secret until he knew one way or another what the future held.

Either he would spend the rest of his life in debtors' prison…

Or Charlotte would have to choose between losing all hope of gaining a respectable reputation, or deciding she would be better off with an annulment than leg-shackled to criminally unlucky Anthony Fairfax.

Fear slithered down his spine. For Charlotte, only one of those outcomes led toward the future she'd dreamed of having.

But he had to try. If he made it through Saturday, he would be on a new path. Once gaol was no longer on the agenda for Monday, he would be able to tell her about the year-long deal he'd struck with Lambley.

And hope that Charlotte would consider staying wed… even if it meant losing what was left of her reputation.

Chapter 21

On Sunday morning, Charlotte watched the rising sun with growing alarm from the bay window of the Fairfax townhouse.

The night before, Anthony had left without telling her where he was going. He'd said he didn't want to worry her or to give her false hope, but that he would be back by daybreak—possibly with good news. Possibly not.

Well, it was daybreak. The streaks of pink through the foggy gray meant, like it or not, Sunday morning had arrived at last. Charlotte gripped a pillow to her chest. She would definitely welcome some good news. Otherwise tomorrow would be her last day with Anthony until she saved enough to set him free.

She glanced at the necklace and earrings lying next to her on the window cushion. Anthony was only willing to sell them as a last resort, and this definitely qualified. First thing tomorrow morning, if all hope was gone, she would force him to go straight to the pawnbroker. She would beg both of their mothers to sell their jewels as well. Charlotte would march to the closest barber and have him shave her cursed gold locks to make into a wig, if it would help raise a few pence.

Anything. Everything. She couldn't lose Anthony.

She loved him.

With a little moan, she leaned the side of her head against the cold windowpane. Her heart was heavy with fear.

How had it come to this? If she lost him tomorrow, her life would still be a hundred times better than it had been a mere fortnight ago, before she had met him. Her relationship with her mother had never been better. Charlotte even had a purpose now. A trade. Society women who complimented her and pleaded for her company. It should all feel like a dream come true.

And yet none of it would matter if she didn't have Anthony to share it with.

Wheels rumbled onto the street. Quickly, she lifted her head from the window. Her smile fell. Not Anthony. This was a fancy coach-and-four with a crest on the side, not a humble hackney cab.

Yet when the carriage stopped, who should alight but her missing husband? Her heart leaped. She scrambled off the window cushion and dashed to the front door to welcome him home.

He didn't look up as he neared the door. Her excitement dimmed. His shoulders were hunched and his feet dragged with every step.

He didn't look as if he bore good tidings. He

looked exhausted. Resigned.

When he saw her waiting in the open doorway, however, his tired green eyes lit with pleasure. He jogged the final steps up the walkway and swung her into his arms.

"We did it," he murmured into her hair. "We *did* it, darling. In a year, we may truly be free."

She gripped his arms. "Did what? How?"

He settled her on one of the few chairs and pulled another close to sit across from her. He ran a hand through his hair and fell into his seat. His countenance was tired, but happy.

"I was at the Duke of Lambley's," he began.

Her breath caught in sudden understanding. "The fancy carriage!"

He nodded as he loosened his cravat. "I've accepted a position. It's not precisely the apprenticeship I was hoping for, but the wages will settle my debts."

She frowned in confusion. "The duke is your employer?"

"Indeed." Anthony's crooked smile did not quite reach his eyes. "I'm to be his night butler on the evenings in which he holds his masked soirées."

"His… what?" she asked faintly.

"Lambley has agreed to settle my outstanding debts in exchange for a year of employment. I'm to replace his butler."

Joyous disbelief rushed through Charlotte's veins. "Butler" was no doubt far from the respectable apprenticeship Anthony had been looking for, but surely any help given to a duke would be a positive step. Especially if he would help Anthony settle his debts.

"Truly? We're free?"

"Not completely. I cannot skip a single shift and, while I am working, I cannot miss a single detail. If I do not perform to the letter of the contract, Lambley has the right to remand me to debtors' prison at once. He will not hesitate to do so, should it be warranted." Anthony leaned forward to take her hands in his. "It will not be easy. I'll understand if trusting me to be responsible for that long is too much of a risk for you to take. There is another way out, but… I don't want to annul this marriage because I don't want to lose you. But I also cannot ask you to spend an entire year suffering the same uncertainty as you have over the last two weeks."

"I'm still in a state of uncertainty," she said, bewildered. Anthony's explanation seemed contradictory… and as though he was leaving important parts out. "What exactly has happened? What will happen next?"

"I've just come from the Cloven Hoof. Lambley went with me after his masquerade to make good on his promise. No more debt collectors. That contract is paid." Anthony squeezed her hands. "I'm not going to Marshalsea. Not today, anyway. I'm not going anywhere, except to work when he summons me and then straight home to you. One year from today, I'll be truly free. Whether you're willing to wait that long is up to you. Until my year is done, there is risk of breach of contract. I shall not blame you if you prefer an annulment."

Her spine went weak. She wouldn't lose him on Monday after all. They had been granted a reprieve.

Yet he could not promise not to fall prey to his gambling weakness again. And the terms of his new contract were alarmingly subjective. What if they found themselves back in the same circumstances once more?

Charlotte straightened her spine. A pragmatic woman would take the annulment. A year of uncertainty would not be easy. But she was no longer powerless. She was in love. Her place was by Anthony's side, now and forever. She threw herself into his arms and held on tight. She would cherish each day as if it were their last.

"I'm not going anywhere," she informed him. "And neither are you."

He covered her face with kisses.

She grinned up at him happily. They would make the best of this situation and anything else life chose to throw at them. "What kind of schedule must you keep? Will it be difficult?"

He pulled a face. "There's no schedule. When Lambley decides to host a party, I must man the door and the books. Perhaps every week during the Season, and every month when London is less crowded." He pressed her hands in his. "I need to make sure you understand something important. This is not… it's not a *respectable* job. What standing I once had in society will be lost by this afternoon. Rumors of my scandalous new employment will be common knowledge by morning." His eyes were haunted. "I know how badly you want to be accepted by society, but from this point forward, any association with me will worsen your reputation, rather than aid it."

She stilled and let his words wash through her. The idea of being respected was still so new, the experience so magical. And it might already be over? Her hopes fell. The year of uncertainty now looked very bleak indeed. As did the lifetime of renewed denigration that would follow.

"I shan't see a single shilling for a full year," he continued. "I cannot offer you a palace, or sumptuous apparel, or nights at the opera. I can no longer even offer you my good name. It will be synonymous with scandal. Under such circumstances, I cannot force you to give up your dreams to be with me. Be honest with yourself about the future you want. We have not yet consummated our marriage. You can still get an annulment if you would be happier without me."

Her throat grew thick. When she had felt her lowest, when Anthony had easily accepted her despite her history and faults, she hadn't given his opinion weight because she had believed the only judges of character were those in high society. She'd been willing to chase an illusion all the way to Scotland rather than look inside herself to find her own worth and meaning.

Charlotte was horrified to think she had affected him in the same way as those who had disparaged her had hurt her.

Anthony was the only one that mattered.

She twined her arms about his neck and gazed deep into his eyes. "I don't give a button what society says. About you, about me. The only thing I care about is us. And if the one thing keeping this marriage from being permanent is consummation…" She curved her lips into a suggestive smile. "How exhausted are you?"

"Not that exhausted." With a growl, he swung her up into his arms and strode straight to their bedchamber.

Her heart raced as he laid her in the center of the bed. This act would prove her love and her commitment. It might also prove that she truly was a whore's daughter. The reality of what was about to happen sent shivers of doubt along her spine. She could never control her body's attraction to him. Perhaps it was she who was about to disappoint him.

Anthony was her husband. Wives were expected to lie with their husbands. What wives *weren't* expected to do was enjoy the encounters. Marital unions were business decisions, political mergers, or even accidents of Fate. They weren't for love, and they certainly weren't for passion.

That's what mistresses were for. Courtesans. Whores.

People like Charlotte.

Right now, her husband was backlit by the embers of the small fire as he tugged off his boots, his greatcoat, his cravat. He wasn't simply an attractive man. He was handsome as sin.

She wished *her* hands were the ones pushing the tailored blue waistcoat off those broad shoulders. She wished *her* fingers were the ones freeing the laces of his undershirt, then lifting it up over his hard stomach, tugging each sleeve from his strong arms, perhaps even touching her lips to his warm bare flesh as he had done to her mere days earlier.

But these weren't the thoughts of a wife. Such carnal desires weren't the idle musings of a gently bred lady or a respectable debutante or an innocent bride.

These were the shamelessly indecent thoughts of a woman who knew full well what sort of blood pulsed in her veins. She took one look at her husband and was filled not with thoughts of demure submission, but with a painful yearning to know him as intimately as possible.

She wanted him heart, soul, and body. But she didn't want him to think of her as a whore. Losing Anthony's respect would be a worse hell than any degradation she'd ever experienced.

He met her eyes and smiled.

She tried to smile back.

Only a demure lady earned a gentleman's respect. And only a brazen trollop without the slightest inhibitions would deserve his passion. The problem was, she couldn't have it both ways.

She was going to have to decide whether she wanted his days—or his nights. Whether she wanted a marriage of respectability… or of passion.

Wearing nothing but his breeches, he crawled into bed beside her and touched a knuckle to her cheek. "I was so worried that this would be the last time I would ever come home to you again."

Unable to speak, she leaned her cheek into his touch and nodded. She, too, had been consumed by the very real probability of him walking into prison and never coming out. That was why she had been curled against the cold window wrapped in a robe, waiting for him to return one last time. Afraid of losing him forever.

She pulled him to her. Having him beside her on

the bed was no longer enough. She needed to feel his warmth next to her skin, and feel his weight pressing against her. She didn't have to feel adrift any longer. He was here. He was hers. It was past time to prove that she was his.

"Kiss me," she commanded. Her voice trembled. There would be no undoing this act.

He immediately complied, enveloping her in his strong embrace and claiming her mouth with his.

Her fingers tangled in his hair as she surrendered to the kiss. The bedchamber was suddenly over warm. He was *here*. She wanted him everywhere. Inside her body. Inside her heart.

She tried to wriggle out of her robe without breaking contact. Anthony seemed to realize what she wanted and peeled the garment from her shoulders without ceasing his kisses.

Charlotte was glad to be rid of the robe. Today she could not bear to have even the thin linen of her night rail or the soft nankeen of his breeches between them.

She lifted the hem of her night rail and pulled it up over her head to flutter to the floor. Never before had she bared herself so completely to any man.

Never before had she trusted anyone enough to risk being vulnerable.

"Remove your breeches," she ordered him, breathless with the knowledge of her own nakedness.

"No," he said as he covered her body with his. "I shall not remove them until I have pleasured you first."

She frowned at this assertion. "I would say you always bring me pleasure."

"I would say you haven't the least idea what pleasure truly is." A wicked smile curved his lips. "But you're about to find out."

Before she could argue, he slanted his mouth over hers and robbed her of all ability to think. Her world had narrowed to only him. His heat. His scent. The taste of his tongue against hers.

He cupped her breast in his large hand. Her nipples immediately grew taut. He took one between his fingers and teased it gently, expertly. She could not help but arch into his touch. Her body was just as drawn to him as her heart.

He broke their kiss, only to lower his mouth to her breast.

An almost painful arousal began to pulse between her legs, swelling, tightening. A longing for something she couldn't quite define, but urgently desired.

Still suckling her breast, he slid his hand down her stomach and cupped her exactly where she had ached to feel his touch. When his fingertip slipped inside her, she realized she was slick with arousal.

There would be no concealing how desperately she wanted his touch. Already her body was writhing into his hand, forcing each stroke of his finger ever deeper with each upward tilt of her hips.

She wanted to freeze, wanted her body to behave like that of a lady instead of a strumpet, but his teeth were grazing her nipple and his fingers were driving into her and his thumb—good heavens, his *thumb*—was circling and flicking and teasing in such a way that she couldn't think, she couldn't breathe, she couldn't stop the sudden explosion of pleasure curling her toes and sending aftershocks of delicious contractions reverberating through her body.

When at last her racing heart had calmed enough for her to realize that she had just wantonly found release on his fingers, before he'd even had the opportunity to remove his breeches, a deep flush of shame rose like fire to her skin. She had exposed her true nature.

Now he would know the truth about who he had wed. She was not a lady. Would never be anything except what she'd been born to be. She was just a—

He covered her mouth with his, each kiss more demanding than the last. Further thought failed her. His breath was as ragged as hers, his skin hot and his muscles taut. Once again, she was lost in his embrace. Swept up in their mutual desire.

"You are the most sinfully irresistible woman I have ever known," he panted as he struggled to loosen his breeches between kisses. "I knew you were perfect before, but every day you prove it just a little more. I am truly the luckiest man alive to have you as my wife."

Her breath caught. Warmth flooded her heart. At her most vulnerable, at her most naked, her most shameless, her most brazen, when he looked at her, he didn't see her past. He saw her future. He didn't see a light-skirt's daughter before him. He saw his wife.

She pulled him to her and wrapped her legs about his now-bare hips and clutched him close as he carefully slid within her. Every thrust of his hips was a promise for the future. Now that they were finally joined as one, she would never let him go.

This was a man worth living for. Worth loving.

Worth spending the rest of her life astonishing and delighting him as often as he astonished and delighted her. Anthony was more than a husband. He was the man she would never stop loving. She would never hold herself back from him again.

From this day forward, they belonged to each other—body and soul.

That was, as long as his contract with the Duke of Lambley didn't rip them apart. Or the Courteland family. Once the duke's will was read, the other family members would learn of her existence.

They could demand the return of their family heirlooms before she could sell them. They were also powerful enough to make her life a living hell. Perhaps even interject themselves in Anthony's fragile, subjective new contract.

If the Courteland family wished to rid themselves of an illegitimate relation, exerting their considerable influence to drive her and Anthony from town would also send him straight to gaol.

Now that they finally had a way out of his mess, were they on the precipice of losing everything all over again?

Chapter 22

The following day, the Duke of Courteland's sprawling London residence loomed before Charlotte like a forbidden palace. Trepidation skittered along her skin. She hesitated before allowing the jarvey to hand her out of the hackney.

Anthony hadn't been allowed to join her for the reading of the will. The meeting was only for named parties and their solicitors. Charlotte's limbs were heavy with worry. After never having been important enough to attract the duke's interest during his lifetime, she still could not believe she'd been mentioned at all.

The duke's true family must have been disgusted to see her name on the list. They would not want someone like her to step one foot into their respectable midst, much less possess any part of their inheritance. Her stomach roiled at the impending debacle. How they must hate her. She needed to steel herself for anything.

She took several deep, calming breaths and stepped away from the hackney cab. By concentrating on nothing more than holding her head high and taking one determined step at a time, she managed to narrow the distance to the duke's imposing front door. Everything about the ornate trim, the spotless windows, the endless garden, reminded her she didn't belong.

And yet here she was.

As she neared the door, a short man with a scuffed beaver hat and a slight limp leaped onto the path beside her.

She froze in place, her heart hammering, and tried to catch her breath. He must have been leaning against one of the many trees, just out of sight—especially to a woman so focused on keeping her feet in motion that she had blocked out the rest of the world.

"Miss Devon," he said with a bow. "That is, Mrs. Fairfax. How do you do this lovely afternoon?"

"I am well, thank you." She did not offer her hand. Now that her heart had calmed, she recognized the man as Mr. Underwood, the solicitor who had followed her from Scotland to Nottingham to inform her that her dead father had named her in his will.

He stepped closer. "Have you given any thought to my proposition?"

She hadn't given any thought to him at all. Nor would she. "What proposition?"

"To manage your funds, should you receive any. To represent you at the reading of the will, and argue on your behalf, should the family cause trouble." His lip curled. "You can be assured they will. The duke's elder sister is an implacable harridan. Believes herself queen. The whole of London trembles before that harpy. They even call her 'the old dragon' when she's not close enough to overhear."

Charlotte shivered. How was she to keep her defenses intact in the presence of someone even her *betters* feared?

"You'll be present for the reading of the will?" she asked.

He lowered his hat. "As your personal solicitor, I wouldn't miss a single word."

"Are you not the personal solicitor to the new duke?" she asked in confusion. A sudden thought occurred to her. "*Is* there a new duke?"

The solicitor cleared his throat. "There is, indeed. He is still being fetched from overseas."

"Then why should you wish to help me? Won't the new duke be your employer?"

Mr. Underwood's lip twisted. "My employment was with the duke himself, not his estate. He wasn't even cold before the old dragon sacked me."

Ah. Charlotte curled her hands into fists. Only those with an ulterior motive ever showed kindness to one such as her. He had offered to help solely as a means to regain access to the dukedom and its masters.

She moved closer to the door. "You have wasted your time. I am not in the market for a solicitor at this moment."

"Then who shall manage your funds?" he asked quickly. A crafty smile twisted his lips. "Your husband? I'm sure he'd enjoy losing every penny at the gaming tables."

She paused with her hand on the knocker.

What if she *did* inherit money today? It would not be hers for long. Not when a wife's husband was sole owner and administrator of all property. Her inheritance wouldn't belong to her, but to Anthony. The solicitor was partially right—any coins in Anthony's pockets hadn't stayed there for long. But Anthony had changed. That senseless wager with the rutting sheep had made him realize how foolish he had been. Since that moment, he hadn't bet so much as a ha'penny.

Yet a cold sweat trickled down the back of her neck. Her husband's lack of control with money had nearly ruined both their lives, and was not yet over. Until he repaid the Duke of Lambley, the specter of debtors' prison continued to cast its shadow over their future and their marriage. An unexpected windfall could send him straight back to the gaming tables—and to ruin.

She couldn't let that happen.

Anthony was unquestionably the last person who should control a single farthing of their money—yet, legally, he was the only person who could.

Unless a solicitor managed some portion of the process. Who did she trust more?

In a gaming hell, there was no fortune too big to be lost forever on the turn of a card. London was full of a thousand such opportunities. To a man who loved to wager, temptation would be everywhere. She could not swallow her dread. Had she come this far only to lose it all? To lose Anthony… If not today, then tomorrow or the next day? And all their money with him?

She glanced over her shoulder at Mr. Underwood.

He placed his hat against his chest. "It would be an honor to protect your interests."

An honor. She laughed without humor. This man would not protect anyone but himself. No one cared about her interests other than Charlotte herself… and Anthony. She would simply have to trust him. And hope for the best.

She turned back to the door and rapped the knocker against its base.

The door swung open to reveal an impassive butler in impeccable attire. "May I help you?"

"I am expected," she stammered. Her neck heated. "My name is Mrs. Fairfax now, but it should be on the list as Charlotte Devon."

The butler held out his hand expectantly.

She stared at him blankly, then colored in humiliation. "I—I don't have a calling card. It's just… Charlotte Devon. It should be on the list."

"See?" whispered Mr. Underwood from behind her. "You need an advocate. These heights are far above your station."

She ground her teeth. He probably *was* just trying to help. Despite his methods, he hadn't had to track her all the way to Scotland just to let her know she'd been named in a will. She doubted the Courtelands thanked him for his interference. She was definitely overreaching her station.

The butler motioned her inside. "One moment."

She took a deep breath and stepped into the manor. The door silently swung closed behind her.

"Wait here." The butler crossed the hall and entered what Charlotte presumed to be a parlor. She could not see within, but the hum of voices was unmistakable.

"*Who?*" shrilled a voice. "Over my dead body. We cannot possibly entertain admittance to my uncle's *bastard*. Toss the rubbish out at once. We shall not compound his mistakes with our own."

Charlotte's cheeks burned with shame. This was what she had expected. Only a fool would let it hurt. She wrapped her arms about herself and wished Anthony could be with her. Perhaps she did need an advocate. Or a hackney cab, to flee while she still could.

"Her name is on the will, Mabel," snapped a cold female voice. "Your disgust with the association does not signify. This is a legal matter, not a family one. Show her in, Teagle."

Charlotte winced. She was not surprised that an illegitimate daughter would not be considered family.

"As you wish, madam."

Within moments, the butler reappeared in the entryway. "If you'll come this way, please."

Humiliation hunching her shoulders, Charlotte concentrated on her breathing and forced her heavy feet to carry her toward the parlor.

"But a *by-blow* isn't *legal*. It's an outrage!" The shrill voice climbed even higher. "You cannot be serious, Aunt. It's a humiliation to us all. This Devon creature is nothing more than the spawn of a—" The voice choked off as Charlotte stepped into the room. "*You?*"

She flung a shocked gaze toward the solicitor. "Charlotte Devon is Mrs. *Fairfax?*"

Charlotte's limbs stopped working. Her face flooded with renewed embarrassment. The outspoken family member so offended at the thought of a whore's daughter in their midst was none other the baroness who had sought her advice not five days prior.

"Lady Roundtree," she said weakly. "How lovely to see you again."

The baroness stared at her openmouthed, then harrumphed and lifted her nose in the air.

"Mabel, that will do," snapped a majestic older lady who sat in an ornate chair. "You will hold your tongue if you wish to attend this meeting. I shall deal with your impertinence later."

The old dragon, Charlotte realized. This was the "dragon lady" Mr. Underwood had warned struck fear into all of London. No wonder Charlotte's entire body trembled. She was about to be eaten alive.

"Sit," the dragon lady commanded. "Mr. Gully will commence with the reading of the will."

Charlotte stumbled over to the empty chair closest to the doorway and forced herself to sit.

Besides Mr. Gully, the only other person in the room was an elegant older lady who fanned her narrow face impatiently, as if both Charlotte and Lady Roundtree were wasting her time.

Dismissing them all, the dragon lady turned her attention to the executor. "Gully, you may begin."

The solicitor cleared his throat. "Thank you all for coming today. While we had anticipated the new duke's presence for the reading of the bequests, he has not yet reached England. However, as his name is not mentioned in the late duke's will, we may continue without worry."

Charlotte's mouth dropped open. "The new duke won't inherit anything?" she blurted.

"Besides the dukedom…?" the elegant lady drawled from behind her painted fan.

The back of Charlotte's neck prickled. Once again she had embarrassed herself. How much proof did she need that their world was not hers?

"The majority of the estate is entailed." The dragon lady's sharp voice carried as she gave the curt explanation. "Courteland was therefore reduced to providing a few monetary disbursements from his private funds."

Charlotte nodded dumbly. Entailed property was so foreign to her experience, it hadn't even crossed her mind. She shrank back in her chair. The thought of being "reduced" to mere pots of money was equally ludicrous. These circles were far above her station indeed. Her fingernails dug into her palms. She didn't belong here at all.

The solicitor lifted a sheaf of parchment. "To the duke's elder sister, Lady Dorothea Pettibone, His Grace the Duke of Courteland leaves all monies not otherwise specified in this document, and grants her the power to oversee all of the following bequests."

The other two ladies gasped. The dragon lady merely inclined her regal head. Clearly this turn of events was nothing less than what she'd expected. A tithe to appease her.

Not the "dragon lady," Charlotte reminded herself. Lady Pettibone had a name. Charlotte would be wise to remember it.

"To the duke's younger sister, Lady Adelia Upchurch, His Grace the Duke of Courteland leaves an annuity of four thousand pounds for the remainder of her life."

Four… thousand… Charlotte's jaw dropped at the exorbitant sum. *Annually.*

"To the duke's niece," the solicitor went on, "the Honorable Lady Mabel Baroness Roundtree, His Grace the Duke of Courteland leaves a single payment of five thousand pounds."

"Not an annuity?" Lady Roundtree choked out in affront. "What did I ever do to deserve such shabby treatment?"

"You've a wealthy husband," Lady Upchurch pointed out dryly. "Isn't your current portion far greater than five thousand pounds?"

Lady Roundtree sniffed. "One can never have too much money."

"To the duke's daughter, Miss Charlotte Devon," the solicitor continued, "His Grace the Duke of Courteland leaves an annuity of one thousand pounds for the rest of her life."

Charlotte's jaw dropped in disbelief. A thousand pounds. *For the rest of her life.* Her heart thudded. The sum was unthinkable.

"Mrs. Fairfax," she stammered inanely. "I'm Mrs. Fairfax now."

"Mrs… Fairfax?" Lady Upchurch repeated, as if tasting the name on her tongue. She turned to Lady

Roundtree with surprise. "Is this the woman you claimed was an angel sent to earth because she performed nothing short of a miracle organizing your downstairs staff?"

Lady Roundtree glared back stonily.

Lady Upchurch arched a disbelieving eyebrow toward Charlotte.

"The very one," Charlotte admitted, peering up through her lashes with an embarrassed smile.

"There," Lady Pettibone said briskly, her impatience clear. "Surely no Courteland has hubris enough to blame an angel for the sins of her father. Do you disagree, Mabel? Are you qualified to cast the first stone?"

Lady Roundtree shook her head mutely. The apples of her cheeks turned pink.

Charlotte could not gloat over witnessing a baroness being put squarely in her place. Her head was still spinning at the sum she had just received. One thousand pounds was enough for a non-society family to live quite comfortably. *More* than enough. She tried to catch her breath. How would she ever spend so much money? Her mother had no debts, or Charlotte would pay them off without blinking an eye. Anthony—

Anthony! This would shorten his contract with the Duke of Lambley. Next year, perhaps, they could rent a small cottage in the country. Such simple accommodation would not be the life Anthony had hoped for, but it would have to do.

She let out a shallow breath. 'Twas actually far better than she had dared to dream.

"How did the duke learn of my existence?" she

asked in a small voice.

"He always knew," Lady Pettibone replied flatly.

Charlotte's heart fell. Her father hadn't been ignorant of her existence. He simply hadn't cared.

Lady Pettibone's tone was imperious. And angry. "I, however, only learned of the matter after my brother took ill."

Charlotte glanced up.

"I came to his bedside to oversee the final draft of his will," Lady Pettibone's expression was implacable. "Because I saw no mention of Mother's ruby necklace or earrings, I inquired as to their whereabouts. When Courteland confessed he had given them to the mother of his illegitimate daughter, I was shocked not to have learned of his indiscretion earlier."

Charlotte flinched at the description. She had spent her life fighting to be seen as someone of value. Even now, after inheriting a stunning annuity, she was still nothing more than a mere indiscretion.

She lifted her chin. The devil could take the lot of them! She didn't care about their high-flown opinions or their world-weary lack of interest. She was a person whether the Courteland clan cared to acknowledge her or not. If her esteemed "betters" had no use for her, well, the feeling was mutual. She didn't need their approval.

"And we were all humiliated to learn he'd been careless enough to let an indiscretion bear fruit," Lady Roundtree muttered.

Lady Pettibone cast a cold eye at her niece. "While a by-blow is not in fact a legal relation, a family such as ours must meet our obligations." She looked down her nose. "I handed Courteland that quill, and informed him that he would fulfill his responsibility, by God, even if it was on his deathbed."

Charlotte's chin jutted defiantly. "Thank you, my lady. No one appreciates your attention to obligations more than I do."

"You were Courteland's responsibility," Lady Pettibone corrected. Her hard eyes softened. "You're my niece. You may not have known your father while he was alive, but now that he's gone… in my home, you will always be welcome to call. I hope you do."

Shock stole the breath from Charlotte's lungs as she stared at Lady Pettibone in amazement. And in hope.

Of all the fashionable people who had disdained and belittled her, these were the individuals who should despise her the most. She was an embarrassment. She had no legal claim to the duke, yet had been bequeathed money that would otherwise have gone to them. She was a bastard. A whore's worthless mistake.

And yet the most feared dragon in all of London was willing to welcome her into her home. To Lady Pettibone, a by-blow wasn't an unfortunate responsibility—she was her niece.

Charlotte's throat stung at the unexpected kindness. Perhaps she wasn't worthless after all.

Perhaps she was family.

Chapter 23

In a daze, Charlotte left the Courteland estate. She was so focused on scanning the street for potential hackney cabs that at first she didn't even register the smart black barouche at the end of the walk, with its beautiful open carriage and gorgeous matched horses.

That was, until her husband leaped down from his perch to swing her into a sweeping kiss.

"Anthony?" She gazed up at him breathlessly. "What are you doing with a barouche?"

"Celebrating!" He swung her up and into the carriage. "Borrowed it for the rest of the afternoon."

She blinked in surprise. "Celebrating? But I haven't even told you—"

"Not the Courtelands. I don't care a fig what those uppity matrons think you're worth." He pulled himself up onto the seat beside her and kissed the tip of her nose. "I know your true value. You're worth everything. And I'd like to prove it to you."

"To prove… what?" she stammered in surprise.

Rather than reply, he shook the reins and set the carriage in motion.

She laughed in delight as the wind fluttered her bonnet and chapped her cheeks. Until this past week, she'd never ridden in a conveyance more prestigious than a humble hackney cab. And even that wasn't a privilege she took for granted.

She'd thought the baroness's fine coach-and-four would be the pinnacle of her elegant travel memories, but this—*this!* The sun on her face, the wind in her hair, the warmth of her husband at her side as the horses clopped smartly into Mayfair and down Upper Grosvenor Street.

When an expansive, bustling garden appeared at the end, she turned to her husband in wonder. He had remembered her childhood dream.

"Hyde Park?" She clasped her hands to her chest and laughed in pure joy. "We're going riding in Hyde Park?"

"Where else does a gentleman take a lady?"

Before she could remind him she was nothing of the sort, they were already inside the park and entering the legendary cavalcade known as the Ring. She tamped down her bonnet to hide her face.

Fashionable people filled the park. Charlotte's eager eyes could scarcely drink it all in. Dashing gentlemen in splendid driving clothes. Elegant ladies in sumptuous day dresses, eye-catching feathers, glorious spencers. Even the liveried servants were the very picture of impeccable taste and unparalleled style.

She tried to stare everywhere all at once. "How many people are here?"

"A thousand, perhaps." Anthony grinned at her obvious delight. "It's mid-afternoon. By six, there will barely be room to move and you will be begging me to leave at once due to your boredom with it all."

"Ha!" She smacked his elbow. Now that she was Mrs. Fairfax, the wife of a town gentleman, she would *never* beg him to leave. This experience was thrilling. She hoped to stay until they were the very last carriage left on the graveled path. As long as she stayed out of sight, she could almost pretend she belonged.

To her surprise, Anthony pulled the barouche to a stop at the inner edge of the Ring and leaped out to the grass below.

"*Anthony*," she hissed as she gripped the side of the barouche to stare down at him in consternation. A few of the fine ladies and gentlemen with painted crests on their carriages gave them curious glances as they passed. She tried to avoid eye contact with them. "What are you doing?"

"Charlotte Fairfax," he called out loud as he dropped to one knee amidst the crowd. "We may have wed by accident, but our marriage is no mistake. You are the love of my life and I would do it all over again. In fact, I'd like to." He gazed up at her and raised his voice even louder. "Will you do me the honor of accepting my hand in marriage, in a proper ceremony before God, with both our families present?"

She gripped the edge of the barouche even tighter

as tears pricked her throat. Blast the romantic man. He'd brought her amongst the *crème de la crème* in London… to choose *her.*

"I love you, Charlotte Fairfax. I love your quick mind and your big heart." He cocked his head and pretended to think. "I even love the snorts you make in your sleep and the way you have no sympathy whatsoever for the stains ruining another pair of my breeches right before your eyes."

She burst out laughing and reached out to him. So what if the smart set were watching? Let them witness the treasure Charlotte had discovered. The man she would spend forever with.

"I love *you*, Anthony Fairfax. I choose you of my own free will. I love the way you make me laugh and keep me safe. There is no one else with whom I would prefer to be accidentally wed. I shall be proud to call myself your wife for the rest of our lives."

With a grin, he sprang back into the carriage and brought her fingers to his lips. "I'd kiss you until you gasped for air, but such behavior is considered scandalous amongst this crowd. Perhaps I can tempt you into returning to the townhouse?"

"I've a better idea." She pulled the folded bequest from her reticule and handed the document to Anthony. "How about we find a townhouse to rent and celebrate somewhere private?"

He stared up from the papers in shock. "One thousand pounds? Per *annum*?"

She blinked at him innocently. "That should be enough to commission a bedchamber, don't you think?"

"If not, there's always the Kitty and Cock Inn," he suggested with a wink.

"Mmm," she murmured as she laid her head on his shoulder. "I did enjoy the Cock Inn."

"The lady's wish is my command." He snapped the reins to set the horses in motion.

Charlotte giggled, then looped her arm through his and smiled in farewell at the sea of fashionable people blurring by. She no longer yearned to be part of their world.

She had everything she needed right there.

Chapter 24

Anthony sat at the head of the crowded dining table in his and Charlotte's new townhouse and grinned at all the family members who had joined them for their wedding breakfast.

His radiant bride, of course. His mother-in-law. His parents. His sister, Sarah, and her husband, Edmund. Even his twin nephews were in attendance, although they appeared far more interested in sucking their thumbs than in the aromatic foodstuffs that crowded the dining table.

Sarah looked up from the boys. "You have a delightful home."

"I have my wife to thank for that." Anthony sent a loving glance across the table at Charlotte.

She shook her head. "We have my inheritance to thank for the townhouse. I have *Anthony* to thank for everything in it."

His mother raised her brows. "Did you win a large

wager?"

"I refused to touch a single penny," he said blandly. He wasn't surprised by the question. His propensity for gambling had never been a secret. "When Charlotte insisted married couples should share all windfalls equally, I spent the next fortnight researching investment opportunities."

"He picked steam-powered cotton mills. He doubled his outlay within a month." Charlotte's voice filled with pride. "He is a genius."

"I'm lucky," he corrected. "You're the genius. Tell them how you saved Lady Grenville's life by helping her to decide whether or not to purchase a puppy."

She grinned back at him. "There are now *two* book clubs vying for my membership."

"Soon we shall require a second basket for calling cards." He gestured over his shoulder toward the fireplace.

Because the wedding had been for family only, the mantel had already begun to collect cards from well-wishers. Every lady Charlotte had ever helped had sent their regards. Anthony's friends had also joined in the fun. Even Maxwell Gideon had written a letter of congratulations, as well as a note offering fifty pounds' credit at the Cloven Hoof.

Anthony had chuckled and thrown temptation directly into the fire, where it belonged. There was nothing left to win. Everything he needed, he had right here at this table.

"A toast." Charlotte's mother lifted her glass. "May your luck never cease, your joy never dim, and your hearts always be full."

Eyes twinkling, Anthony's sister Sarah raised her glass. "And may the twins soon be blessed with a pair of cousins to play with."

A grin curved his lips. He could certainly drink to that.

His heart warmed as he met Charlotte's eyes across the table. He had gambled more than any man ought, and won more than any man deserved. He had a wife he adored. Family who supported him. Money he earned honestly, rather than wagered and lost. Friends who sought his time, not his pocketbook.

Happiness filled him. Moments like these were far more than simple good fortune. Anthony wasn't merely the Lord of Chance.

He was loved.

Epilogue

Charlotte gripped the reins tightly in her gloved hands as she steered their shiny new barouche into the cavalcade toward Hyde Park. She sat between her husband and her mother—the two people she loved most. It was only fitting for the three to be together in their new carriage for its very first promenade.

Her mother's lively blue eyes took in their fine surroundings with enthusiasm. She sighed over every nattily dressed lord or lady, and cooed in delight at the spotted Dalmatian carriage dogs accompanying the grandest coaches.

Anthony, however, only had eyes for Charlotte.

It was he who had suggested a drive along the Ring for their barouche's first outing. He who had agreed without hesitation when Charlotte had teasingly asked if she could take the reins.

Now that she had them, holding such power was

exhilarating. Empowering. Terrifying. She wasn't at all certain whether the horses were heeding her command or simply falling into step with the endless stream of carriages.

"Look," her mother whispered. "A gentleman with a painted crest upon his coach has matched our pace, as if he wishes to speak with us."

"I can't look," Charlotte said through gritted teeth as she clutched the reins even tighter. "If I look, I'm liable to swerve right into him."

Anthony tugged the reins from her white-knuckled hands and greeted the gentleman. "Good afternoon, Lambley."

Charlotte's mouth fell open.

"Fairfax." The duke inclined his head toward the ladies. "Mrs. Fairfax. Miss Devon."

He drove off without another word.

Her mother stared in shock. "Did a *duke* just publicly acknowledge us?"

"He probably ruined our reputations by doing so," Anthony assured her. "We're far more respectable than Lambley."

Charlotte shook her head fondly.

Now that Anthony had finished repaying his gambling debts, he had no legal responsibility to keep his position as the night butler for the duke's scandalous masquerades. He claimed he stayed on solely to relieve the duke of his money, but Charlotte rather suspected her husband enjoyed feeling useful. She certainly did. In certain circles, her name was the first to surface when someone was in need of good, sound advice. Not the highest circles, of course. But having circles at all was new to Charlotte. She had friends now. People who didn't shy away from her company.

"Fairfax!" A handsome gentleman with thick golden locks and a brilliant white smile rode up beside them on a black stallion.

"Lord Wainwright." Anthony tipped his hat. "Heading to a ride on Rotten Row?"

"I no longer care about such distractions. You must tell me who the divine creature was in the emerald dress," Lord Wainwright said in hushed tones. "The one in the scarlet plumed mask with the diamond eyeholes. I am desperate."

"I'm afraid I cannot help." Anthony's tone was firm. "Privacy is paramount. If you need to contact a guest from a party, you could consider speaking to the party's host."

Lord Wainwright rubbed the back of his neck and sighed. "He won't tell me. He said you wouldn't either, but I had to try."

Before Anthony could respond, the handsome gentleman cantered off on his stallion, vanishing like a prince from a fairy story.

"Who is Lord Wainwright?" Charlotte asked once the dust had settled behind him.

Anthony grimaced. "Do you remember when you asked me if I knew any scandalous dukes and earls? *That* is the rake I'm delighted you didn't meet before you met me. Wainwright is more than incorrigible. That particular earl has cut quite a swath in the ballrooms—even the masked ones."

She nestled into him. "When shall I be invited to attend one? A masquerade, I mean."

"As long as Wainwright might be there?" Anthony clutched his chest in mock horror. "Never."

"*Charlotte*," her mother hissed, rapping her knee with a fan. "Charlotte, look. I recognize that crest. It belongs to the Duke of Courteland."

As the coach-and-four passed, Charlotte realized one of the ladies inside the carriage was Lady Pettibone, her terrifying dragon aunt. Their eyes met.

Charlotte tensed. Not being evicted should she appear at the lady's private estate was not at all the same as being given leave to acknowledge their tenuous relationship in public. She gave a tentative smile and held her breath.

Lady Pettibone inclined her head. "Mrs. Fairfax."

The breath whooshed out of Charlotte's lungs in relief. "Lady Pettibone. How lovely to see you."

Lady Pettibone's coach pulled farther ahead, and the ladies inside disappeared from view.

Charlotte's mother looked at her in awe. "*Lady Pettibone* greeted you?"

Charlotte lifted a shoulder as if the tense moment hadn't very nearly stopped her heart.

The truth was… it didn't matter who acknowledged her. It had taken her all this time to realize that most of London's inhabitants hadn't the least idea who she was, much less were aware of the circumstances of her birth. Even her mother's once-infamous face no longer raised many brows. Despite the size of this enormous city, Charlotte could spend the majority of her time in relative anonymity.

She was just herself now: Mrs. Charlotte Fairfax.

Giver of advice, and member of lively book clubs everywhere. Now that Anthony was out of debt and they could afford to leave the city, she no longer desired to. There was nothing to escape.

She leaned her head against her husband's strong shoulder in satisfaction. He immediately wrapped his arm about her to hold her close.

Charlotte smiled contentedly. She had friends now. Security for her mother. A much larger family. Nephews she couldn't wait to spoil. A husband who adored her.

Love filled her heart.

She had finally come home.

Acknowledgments

Huge thanks go out to Morgan Edens for her advice, encouragement, and willingness to FaceTime at the drop of a hat to plotstorm with me. You are the best!

My deepest thanks also go to my editors, Jane Hammett and Lesley Jones, whose careful eyes catch everything from typos to continuity goofs. Any mistakes are my own.

Lastly, I want to thank the *Dukes of War* facebook group and my fabulous street team. Your enthusiasm makes the romance happen. I thought of you as I wrote this story.

Thank you so much!

Thank You for Reading

I hope you enjoyed this story!

Sign up at EricaRidley.com/club99
for members-only freebies
and special deals for 99 cents!

Did you know there are more books in this series?

This romance is part of
the *Rogues to Riches*
regency-set historical series.

In order, the *Rogues to Riches* books are:

Lord of Chance
Lord of Pleasure
Lord of Night
Lord of Temptation
Lord of Secrets
Lord of Vice

In order, the *Dukes of War* books are:

The Viscount's Christmas Temptation
The Earl's Defiant Wallflower
The Captain's Bluestocking Mistress
The Major's Faux Fiancée
The Brigadier's Runaway Bride
The Pirate's Tempting Stowaway
The Duke's Accidental Wife

Join the *Dukes of War* Facebook group for giveaways and exclusive content: http://facebook.com/groups/DukesOfWar

Other Romance Novels by Erica Ridley:

Let It Snow
Dark Surrender
Romancing the Rogue

About the Author

Erica Ridley is a *New York Times* and *USA Today* bestselling author of historical romance novels.

In the new *Rogues to Riches* historical romance series, Cinderella stories aren't just for princesses... Sigh-worthy Regency rogues sweep strong-willed young ladies into whirlwind rags-to-riches romance with rollicking adventure.

The popular *Dukes of War* series features roguish peers and dashing war heroes who return from battle only to be thrust into the splendor and madness of Regency England.

When not reading or writing romances, Erica can be found riding camels in Africa, zip-lining through rainforests in Central America, or getting hopelessly lost in the middle of Budapest.

For more information, visit www.EricaRidley.com.